PHANTUM

THE NIGHT PRINCESS

Prologue

The city glowed like temptation. Every streetlight hummed against the dark, bouncing off wet pavement and high heels, tracing the outline of a woman who no longer answered to her old name. They called her Phantum now — the kind of name that made people whisper before they said it out loud. But before the masks, the champagne, and the cameras, she was just Jasmine — a girl who learned the hard way that beauty opened doors and danger kept them shut.

Tonight wasn't about where she came from. It was about who she had become. The mirror caught her reflection in flashes of gold: lips painted with precision, lashes like weapons, eyes cold enough to melt any man's pride. A black mask lay on the vanity beside her — delicate, carved with filigree so fine it seemed to breathe. She stared at it for a moment, fingers brushing the edge. The mask wasn't just decoration; it was survival.

She'd been too real for too long. Too honest in a city that only respected illusion. The mask gave her freedom — a way to walk through fire and still smell like smoke and sin. When she put it on, she wasn't Jasmine anymore. She was legend.

The sound of the elevator chimed in the distance, pulling her out of the mirror's gaze. She grabbed her clutch, straightened her dress, and took one last look at the woman staring back. Power wasn't something you were given; it was something you became. And tonight, she was becoming it.

When the elevator doors opened, the air changed. Flashing lights, camera clicks, murmurs of her name from strangers who thought they knew her story. She didn't flinch, didn't blink, didn't hesitate. She smiled that slow, knowing smile that made the world freeze for half a second.

Because tonight wasn't about who she was — it was about who they believed she'd become.
And that's the real power of a Phantum.

CHAPTER 1

Born in the Fire

Memphis had a sound to it. The streets didn't hum, they rattled — dice hitting concrete, basslines shaking old box Chevys, arguments leaking through thin apartment walls. Sirens were lullabies. Gunshots were punctuation.

That's the city that raised me. That's where I was born — Jasmine Marie Carter, 1992.

Our mama, Denise Carter, was already half-gone by the time I came into the world. She was young, reckless, and drowning herself in liquor, men, and menthols. I wasn't her first mistake. That title belonged to my sister, Keekee.

Keekee was four years older, and she wore those years like armor. Loud. Fast. Always the one talking back, rolling her eyes, daring the world to check her. Where I was quiet, watching everything, Keekee was the storm.

"Lil' Jas, you scared as hell," she told me once, smacking her gum. "You sit around like somebody gon' hand you somethin'. Don't nobody owe us shit. If you want it, you better take it."

I didn't answer. I never did. I just watched her and Mama and the block around us, collecting lessons I didn't even know I'd need.

Mama worked jobs here and there, but nothing stuck. She was better at chasing gin bottles than paychecks. She'd stumble in late, lipstick smeared, heels in her hand, cussing about men or bills or both.

The fridge was always half-empty. When she cooked, it was fried baloney with the red strip curling up in the pan, or greasy chicken wings from the corner store. When she didn't, we drank water and chewed on the edges of stale bread.

One night I asked her why she didn't buy milk. She looked at me through half-shut eyes and said, "Girl, be grateful you got somethin' to drink." That was Mama Denise.

By the time I was eight, and Keekee was twelve, Mama's body was breaking down. She was only in her thirties, but she looked twice that — skin dull, cough heavy, hands shaking. Years of Newports, gin, and pills were catching up.

Our apartment was chaos most nights. Men in and out. Shouting matches. Laughter that turned to sobbing.

I remember one night clear: Mama in the kitchen with some dude whose name I never learned. She was slurring, bottle in her hand. "You don't tell me what the fuck to do!" she screamed.

He shoved her, hard enough to knock her into the counter. She just laughed, lit another cigarette, and waved him out the door. That was Mama, fragile but too stubborn to admit it.

The night she died, it was quiet. No man, no fight. Just her at the table with a bottle and a handful of pills. I was half-asleep in the back when I heard something crash.

"Keekee," I whispered, shaking her. "Mama fell."

Keekee groaned, pulling the blanket over her head. "She always fallin'. Go back to sleep."

But when the sun came up, Mama was still on the kitchen floor. The cigarette in her hand had burned down to the filter, ash scattered across the linoleum. Her lips were blue. Eyes half-open, staring at nothing.

"Mama?" I whispered, shaking her hand. "Mama, wake up." She didn't move.

Keekee came out, saw her, and froze. Then she cursed under her breath, "Shit." She ran next door, banging on the neighbor's door until somebody called 911.

The paramedics came, sirens screaming, down the block. Two men in uniforms knelt beside her, checked her pulse, and shook their heads.

"Overdose," one muttered. "Mix of liquor and pills. Body couldn't take it." I didn't know what overdose meant; all I knew was Mama wasn't coming back.

They buried her in a cheap pine casket with wilted flowers. Hardly anybody came — a couple neighbors, one of her old drinking buddies, and Aunt Laverne.

I sat in the front row, clutching Keekee's sleeve like it was a lifeline. Keekee chewed her gum hard with a tight jaw and muttered, "She ain't never care about us. Now she gone and left us with nothing." I didn't say a word. Just held on, afraid if I let go, I'd disappear too.

That's when Aunt Laverne stepped in. Mama older sister. Church lady with tired eyes and hands rough from years of work. She lived in Atlanta, said she couldn't let us rot in

Memphis. "Pack what you got," she told us. "You comin' with me." What we had was two trash bags of clothes and a shoebox of pictures.

The bus ride was long. Hours of highway, hours of silence. Keekee had headphones in, ignoring me. I stared out the window, watching Memphis shrink in the distance. Aunt Laverne patted my knee. "This a fresh start, baby. Don't waste it." But Keekee only rolled her eyes.

Atlanta wasn't no miracle. Capitol Homes smelled like piss in stairwells too. Same bass shaking car doors. Same corner boys watching with sharp eyes. "Shit whack," Keekee said, looking around. "Memphis niggas realer." But it didn't take long before she had Atlanta boys whistling her name too.

By fifteen Keekee's belly was round. Aunt Laverne cried, fussed, threatened. But Keekee didn't care. She had the baby — a girl with Keekee's pout — and shoved her off on everybody else. "Here, Jas, hold her," she'd say, pushing the baby into my arms before running off with whatever boy was waiting outside.

I rocked my niece, whispering, "Auntie got you," even though I was still a child myself.

Keekee came home late, sometimes with bruises on her arms, lips swollen. She never picked that baby up. "She his problem, not mine," she spat one night when Aunt Laverne begged her to help.

And just like that, the cycle repeated. Mama abandoned us in death. Keekee abandoned her daughter in life. I learned fast: Love don't guarantee nothing. Mothers leave. Sisters fail. Men hurt.

Keekee was lost. Aunt Laverne was tired. And me? I was in the middle, clinging to the pieces, trying not to drown in their shadows. But deep down, I told myself something.
I'll be different. Stronger. Smarter.

I didn't know yet what "different" meant. I just knew I couldn't end up like Mama. And that's when the streets gave me an answer. That answer had a name. CJ.

CHAPTER 2

The Dope Boy's Princess

Keekee always came home glowing like she'd just won the lottery. Hair messy, lips swollen from kissing, eyes glittering like she had a secret. "Jas, you don't even *know*," she said one night, flopping down on the couch while I bounced her baby on my knee. "I met this dude. Chris. He the truth."

I frowned. "Another one?"

She smacked her gum, ignoring my tone. "Nah, same guy, he just do something to me, this ain't like the rest of these broke-ass project niggas. Chris different. He got money, real money. Pulled up in a candy-painted Chevy sittin' on rims so big I had to climb in like a truck. System so loud, the whole block turned their heads."

I rolled my eyes, rocking the baby. "Cars don't mean nothing. Anybody can rent a ride."

Keekee shot me a glare. "Hater. You just mad 'cause don't nobody looking at you like that yet. But wait till you grow into them lil' hips — you gon' see."

I stayed quiet, but her words stung. She wasn't finished. "Chris keep a roll so fat, Jas, I swear it could choke somebody. He be flashing hunnids like it ain't shit. And he told me I'm too fine to be stuck in this hood. Said he gon' put me on." Her voice had that dreamy tilt, the kind you couldn't argue with. I didn't bother trying. I just tucked the name away in my head. *Chris.*

Weeks rolled by, nothing changing, then shit hit the fan. The baby had been crying all damn day. My arms were tired, back sore, but Keekee was nowhere in sight.

When she finally came stumbling in, smelling like weed smoke and some dude's cologne, Aunt Laverne was waiting in the kitchen, arms crossed, robe tied tight.

"'Bout damn time you brought your ass home," Auntie snapped. "This baby been hollerin' since morning. You think you slick, runnin' them streets while we stuck raisin' what you pushed out?"

Keekee rolled her eyes, tossed her jacket on the chair. "Man, chill. She fine. Jas got her."

"Jas is a child," Auntie barked. "You fifteen with a baby and still actin' like you thirteen! You gon' end up just like your mama if you keep this up — dead before your time."

That made Keekee's lip curl. "Don't start with that shit. I ain't Mama. I ain't no drunk ass."

"You worse!" Auntie shot back. "At least Denise kept her kids close. You runnin' out here with niggas like they gon' save you. Don't none of them care 'bout you. And sure as hell none of 'em care 'bout this baby!"

Keekee snatched her purse from the table, eyes blazing. "That baby ain't mine no more!" she screamed. "That's Chris's problem. He the daddy, he need to step up. Y'all want me to play house while he ride clean and stack paper? Fuck that."

The words hit like a slap. I froze, clutching the baby tight against my chest. Auntie's face went pale, then red. "Don't you dare blame no man. That child came out you. You laid down, you made her, now raise her!"

Keekee shook her head hard, tears in her eyes but anger on her lips. "Nah. Y'all want her? Keep her. I'm done." She stormed to the door, yanked it open.

"Keekee!" Auntie shouted, voice cracking. "Don't you walk out that door!" But the door slammed so hard the picture frames rattled on the wall. That was it. No goodbye. No looking back.

The baby whimpered against my chest, tiny fists curled. I rocked her, whispering, "Shhh... Auntie got you."

Aunt Laverne sank into the chair, face in her hands. "Lord, give me strength. First Denise, now this one. I can't do it no more." Her voice broke into sobs, tired and raw.

I held the baby tighter, staring at the door Keekee had slammed. My chest burned with something I didn't have a name for yet...anger, maybe. Abandonment. All I knew was this: Keekee was gone. And she wasn't coming back.

I was thirteen and holding down for whatever family I had left, but I felt like I was standing on the edge of something bigger than myself. My body was changing, and the block noticed before I did.

Booty filling out, thighs getting thick from running up and down them busted Capitol Homes stairs, skin glowing even when I didn't bother with lotion. I'd catch older boys staring when I walked by, their eyes hanging on me longer than they should've.

The older girls in the neighborhood? They noticed too, but their comments were sharp, like knives hidden in laughter. "Lil' Jas out here tryin' to grow a ass," one of them called out on the corner one afternoon, her friends busting out laughing.

"Better tell her keep them lil' hips covered before she end up like Keekee — pregnant and gone." I rolled my eyes and kept walking, but my chest burned. Later that night, sitting on Auntie's porch, I whispered to myself, I ain't gon' end up like Keekee.

Still, I couldn't lie; I felt something humming under my skin. Like a secret power I didn't know how to use yet.

The boys at the basketball court made it obvious. Every time me and Tika walked past, the game slowed down, all eyes swinging our way. "Damn, lil' Jas turnin' into somethin'." "Yo, she thicker than last summer." "Bet she gon' be bad as fuck by sixteen."

I pretended I didn't hear, kept my chin high. But inside, I felt a mix — part anger, part fear, part thrill. They were right about one thing: I wasn't invisible no more.

Sometimes, late at night, I'd stand in front of the cracked bathroom mirror; I'd pull my T-shirt tight around my waist, tilt my head, watch the way my curves showed up. I didn't look like the kid Mama used to braid up before school. I didn't even look like the girl Keekee used to clown for wearing hand-me-downs. I looked like somebody the world was already trying to claim.

"Girl, you better get ready," my cousin Tika laughed one afternoon, popping gum as we braided each other's hair. "You gon' have to fight these niggas off with a stick. Look at you — stomach flat, thighs out here sittin', hair growin' thick. Shit, I'm jealous."

"Shut up," I muttered, but I smiled a little.

"I'm serious," she pressed. "They already whisperin'. They gon' start knockin' soon. Question is, who you gon' let in?"

I shrugged, braiding tighter to avoid answering. But the truth? I didn't know. All I knew was this — I wasn't a child anymore. And the streets could feel it.

The heat that July was suffocating. Even the breeze felt like it came out a damn oven.

Me and Tika were posted at the busted-ass bus stop, sweat soaking through our T-shirts, thighs sticking to the plastic bench. My red Faygo was warm, Tika's braids clung to her neck, and we were both bitchin' about how the bus always came late when you needed it most.

That's when it happened. Bass hit first. Heavy. Low. The kind of bass you felt in your chest before your ears even caught it. A candy-painted box Chevy slid slow around the corner, sitting high on twenty-fours. Chrome rims spinning lazy, windows tinted black. The whole block looked up.

Car stopped at the corner like it was waiting for applause. Then the window slid down smooth, like a curtain pulling back on a stage.

And there he was. Not a boy, not really a man either. Seventeen, maybe eighteen. Fresh shape-up. White tee crisp enough to cut somebody. Gold chain glinting in the sunlight.

His eyes were what got me. Sharp. Heavy. Like he'd already seen enough to know how shit ended. "You dropped somethin'," he said, voice low but clear.

I looked down. A folded twenty sat by my foot. I hadn't dropped a thing. "That ain't mine," I said, straight-faced.

He smirked, leaned back in the driver's seat like he had all the time in the world. "Well, it ain't mine either. Guess somebody should hold it 'til the rightful owner comes back."

Tika giggled, twisting her hair around her finger. "Boy, you corny."

He didn't flinch. Just smirked wider. "Probably. But I'm honest. They call me CJ."

13

He didn't say it like bragging. Didn't need to. He said it like a fact, like a name that mattered whether I liked it or not. "Jasmine," I said, then caught myself. "But everybody call me Jas."

He repeated it slow, letting it sit on his tongue. "Jas." The way he said it made me feel like he was already claiming it.

"You want a lift?" he asked, nodding toward the Chevy. "Bus gon' be another thirty minutes, easy. I can get y'all home quicker."

Tika's eyes lit up like fireworks. She was halfway to the car before I grabbed her arm. "We good," I said.

CJ tilted his head, studying me like I was a puzzle. Then he nodded, calm. "Bet. Respect. But if y'all get tired of waitin', I'll be around." He pulled off slow, rims gleaming, bass fading into the hum of traffic.

Tika turned to me, smacking my arm. "Bitch, what is wrong with you? Did you see that car? Did you see that chain? That man is fine." I kept my face steady, sipping the last of my warm Faygo. But inside? Something was stirring.

The car looked familiar. The face too. Like I'd seen it before, somewhere I couldn't place. But I pushed it down. All I knew right then was this: somebody important had noticed me.

And that felt good. Real good.

CJ wasn't the type you saw once and forgot. Nah. He made sure you remembered.

Couple days after the bus stop, me and Tika were walking back from the corner store, arms full of Now & Laters and hot chips. The Chevy was parked right out front, paint gleaming like it had its own sun. CJ leaned against the hood, chain swinging, sipping a Coke like he owned the sidewalk.

"You eatin' today, Jas?" he called out, eyes on me.

I blinked, shifting the bag in my arms. "I always eat."

He grinned, pulled a small bag of chips from behind his back. "Then eat better." He tossed it to me smooth.

I caught it without thinking, staring down at the crinkled bag in my hands. Tika squealed like she'd just been proposed to. "Oh my God, he bought you chips!" she whispered loud enough for half the block to hear.

I shot her a look. "Girl, shut up." Then to him: "I didn't ask you for this."

"Didn't say you did," CJ replied easy. "Sometimes you don't gotta ask. Real ones just look out."

Tika giggled, twisting her hair. "You a mess. You out here flirtin' with my cousin wit' free snacks?"

CJ smirked. "Snacks today. Whole meals tomorrow. Depend how she act."

My cheeks warmed, but I rolled my eyes hard. "Boy, please. I don't need no man buying me no damn chips."

He shrugged, unbothered. "Good. Then it's just a gift. You can throw it away if you don't want it."

And that's the part that got me. Most dudes on the block pressed too hard, talked too loud, tried too much. CJ? He dropped it in my lap and let me choose.

After that, it was little things. A soda slid across the counter at the store. A ride offered on a hot day. A joke whispered under his breath that only I caught.

CJ never crowded me. He circled. Patient, like a cat playing with a bird. And every time, he left me thinking about him long after he was gone.

"Girl, you acting too tough," Tika teased one night, sprawled on my bed painting her nails. "If you don't want him, I do."

I shot her a glare. "Then take him."

She smirked. "He don't want me. He want you. I can tell by the way he say your name. He say it like it's already his." I stayed quiet, but she wasn't lying. CJ didn't talk to me like I was just another girl on the block. He talked to me like I was different. And that scared me more than it excited me.

It was a Saturday when I finally said yes. Me and Tika were sitting outside Auntie's building, legs swinging off the porch steps, when that Chevy pulled up again. Candy paint gleaming, bass humming low like a heartbeat. CJ leaned out the window, arm draped across the seat. "Bus running today?"

Tika giggled. "Boy, she don't even like the bus no more, she just frontin'."

I shot her a look, then sighed, standing slow. "One ride. That's it."

CJ grinned, chain catching the sun. "Bet."

Sliding into that Chevy felt like stepping into another world. Seats soft, air smelling like cologne and money. Dashboard clean, no trash, no mess. Just order. "Seatbelt," he said, nodding.

I clicked it in place, trying to keep my face calm even though my stomach was flipping. He pulled off smooth, no jerks, no rush. Just confidence. Like the streets opened for him.

We ended up at Lenox Mall, and for me, that was like stepping into a palace. I'd been before with cousins, window-shopping, joking around, but never like this. Never riding shotgun in a box Chevy on 24s, never walking in beside somebody who looked like he belonged there.

People stared. Security guards eyed us. Girls whispered behind their hands. CJ didn't flinch. He walked like he owned the building, arm brushing mine, chin high.

First stop: the sneaker store. He pointed at a pair of white Nikes. "What size you wear?"

I blinked. "Why?"

"'Cause you mine," he said plain. "And my girl don't walk around in no busted-ass shoes." Before I could argue, he told the clerk my size. Box slid across the counter. Cash peeled off his roll like it was nothing.

"Try 'em on," he said. I did. Perfect fit. "You look good in 'em," he said, eyes steady.

My chest warmed, but I rolled my eyes. "Boy, they just shoes."

"Yeah," he smirked. "But on you, they different."

We hit the food court next. He came back with a tray piled high — nuggets, fries, milkshake. Slid it in front of me like he'd been feeding me all his life. "You eat like you ain't ate in a week," he teased, watching me tear into the fries.

"Maybe I haven't," I shot back, mouth full.

He laughed, deep and low, the kind of laugh that stayed in your chest after it was gone. "I like you, Jas. You don't pretend."

Nobody had ever said that to me before. Not like that. On the way out, he stopped at a kiosk, pointed to a thin gold bracelet. "Put that on her," he told the clerk.

I shook my head. "CJ, nah..."

He cut me off. "Queens don't argue about crowns. You mine. You don't walk around empty-handed." The clerk clasped it around my wrist. Light caught on the gold. My fingers trembled, but I didn't take it off.

Walking beside him, I felt eyes on me. Girls staring, boys nodding. For the first time, I wasn't invisible. I was somebody.

On the ride back, he turned the music down low. "You know why I fuck with you, Jas?" he asked, eyes on the road. I shook my head.

"You ain't thirsty like these other hoes. You don't chase. You watch. You listen. That's dangerous."

"Dangerous how?" I asked, voice small.

"Dangerous like you could run shit if you wanted. All you need is somebody to lace you with the rules." I leaned back, staring at my bracelet in the glow of the streetlights. For the first time, I let myself believe him.

That night, lying in bed, I couldn't sleep. The gold bracelet still clung to my wrist. Every time I closed my eyes, I heard his laugh, saw the way people stepped aside when we walked. And deep down, I knew; something had shifted.

The first time I felt the streets breathe down my neck was in CJ's passenger seat.

It was late, maybe 11 p.m., and the city was humming low. Windows down, bass soft, summer air thick. I had my new gold bracelet on, my Nikes still clean, feeling like the whole world was watching me ride shotgun in that candy-painted Chevy.

Then blue lights lit up the rearview. My chest dropped. "CJ…" I whispered.

"Breathe, Jas," he said, voice calm like he'd been here a hundred times. "Don't touch nothin'. Don't say nothin'. Just breathe."

The car rolled to the curb, tires crunching against gravel. The officer's flashlight cut through the dark, slicing across the interior like a blade.

"License and registration." CJ pulled his wallet out smooth, no rush, no shake in his hand. He slid the license forward with a slight smirk, like he'd rehearsed this. I leaned just enough to see it - and froze.

Date of birth. Do the math. He was seventeen. Seventeen.

But the chain, the ride, the way he carried himself? That was no teenager shit. He moved like he was twenty-three, maybe older. Like he'd been grown longer than he'd been alive.

The cop squinted at the license, then at him. "You young to be ridin' like this, son. What you do for a living?"

CJ's smile was quick, polite. "Work with my uncle. Body shop."

The cop stared a beat longer, then shined the light at me. My heart thudded so hard I thought it would crack my ribs. I kept my eyes down, hands folded tight in my lap.

After a pause that stretched like forever, the light clicked off. "Get home safe," the officer said flat. CJ slid the license back in his wallet, waited till the lights disappeared before pulling off.

I let out a breath so hard it shook. "CJ...you seventeen?"

He glanced at me, smirked. "What it say?"

"It say you seventeen. You told me you was grown."

He shrugged, one hand loose on the wheel. "I am grown. Age don't make you a man. How you move make you a man. And I move better than half these thirty-year-old niggas out here."

I stared at him, bracelet glinting in the dash light. And I couldn't lie; he wasn't wrong. Yeah, he was seventeen. But he carried himself like twenty-three. Like he had the world figured out while the rest of us were still learning how to breathe.

"Don't worry 'bout what's on paper," he said, voice low. "Worry 'bout what's in front of you. I told you before — you safe with me. Always." He reached over, resting his hand on my knee. Warm. Steady.

And just like that, the fear melted into something else. Something sharper. Because if he could calm cops with a smile, if he could wear seventeen like it was twenty-three, then maybe he really was untouchable. And maybe I was too, as long as I was with him.

It wasn't just cops watching CJ. The streets watched him too. One afternoon we were leaving Lenox, shopping bags in hand, when a black Cutlass rolled by slow. Windows down, eyes sharp. CJ clocked it without blinking, jaw tightening just enough for me to notice.

"You know them?" I whispered.

He slid an arm around me, steering me toward the garage. "Don't worry about it. Just some niggas hatin' 'cause I shine too bright."

But I saw the way his fingers flexed near his waistband. The way his eyes scanned mirrors. CJ carried himself like twenty-three, but the danger around him aged him even more.

That night, parked under a buzzing streetlight, he turned to me, voice low and certain. "Listen, Jas. You stick with me, you gon' be good. I ain't never lettin' you go hungry, I ain't never lettin' nobody touch you. You mine. That mean somethin'."

The gold bracelet gleamed on my wrist, the night air thick between us. For the first time, I believed him.

Even though part of me — the part that still remembered Mama's body on the kitchen floor and Keekee walking out the door without looking back — whispered that nothing in the streets lasted forever. But I pushed that voice down. Because right then, I wasn't just Jasmine anymore. I wasn't Denise's daughter. I wasn't Keekee's little sister.

I was CJ's. I was the Dope Boy's Princess.

CHAPTER

3

The Game's First Lesson

By the time the leaves started pretending to change — Atlanta's little two-week flirt with fall — I could read a room the way other girls read magazines. Shoes first. Hands second. Silence last.

CJ liked to hold court in the parking lot after dark, music set low like a heartbeat, boys circling the Chevy as if it prayed. I stayed in the passenger seat with the door cracked, legs tucked, hat low. From there I could see everything without being a part of it.

Most nights I was with CJ; Keekee's baby shouldn't be my problem, but I still tried to be around when I could. Aunt Laverne mostly shook her head when I came by to relieve her, so she could go to work.

I wasn't trying to be the loudest girl on the asphalt. I was trying to live long. Tika said I looked like a music video from the neck down and a bank robber from the eyebrows up. "Why you always got that brim pulled like you hiding?"

"I am," I said, and she didn't know how true.

The night it happened didn't start special. CJ washed the Chevy himself, a rag in slow circles like he trusted his hands more than any car wash. I watched the way water beaded and ran; the tiny rivers choosing their own path down paint that looked like wet candy. He talked about nothing and everything, the way men do when they want you close and their mind is somewhere counting other things.

"You hungry?" he asked finally, tossing the rag into the bucket.

"Always," I said. We hit a wing spot where the fryer sang and the air tasted like peppered oil. CJ ordered extra lemon pepper, told the cook to drown the box, and slid it to me with that small proud smile.

He loved to feed me. Maybe because he knew what empty felt like. Maybe because feeding somebody is a way to own a piece of them. I ate until my fingers gleamed and licked the salt from my knuckles. When I glanced up, he was watching like I was a TV show that never missed.

"Don't look at me like that," I said, half-laughing, half-annoyed.

"Like what?"

"Like I belong to you."

He leaned back, grin slow. "You do," he said, soft as a prayer and just as dangerous.

I didn't answer. I tucked that sentence behind my ribs with the other pretty lies and ugly truths I was saving for later.

We slid out to a block where everybody came to be seen. It was a hood-rich parade, mufflers loud enough to wake the past, gold teeth flashing like fish in a shallow river. I stepped out long enough to hug two girls I halfway liked and to let them see the bracelet CJ had bought that week. Then I got back in.

He did his rounds, that calm walk that said he understood the math of territory. Fists, elbows, eyes. He made people feel seen, and that's a kind of currency. He spent it like he'd never run out.

I was watching shoes when I felt the air go thin. Not quieter, just tight, like somebody cinched the night around the waist. Two cars over, a boy in a hoodie left his body before he moved. You could see it in the way his jaw locked, the way his friends gave him space instead of holding him. Trouble announces itself even when it whispers.

I bent toward the dash, adjusted the vent like it mattered. CJ slid back into the driver's seat and didn't start the car. He looked past me — left, right, left again — counting, measuring.

"You good?" I asked, voice level.

"Yeah," he said. Then, "Put your seatbelt on." That was how I knew he wasn't. I clicked the belt. He didn't pull off.

The boy in the hoodie turned into a person with a face I recognized from the wrong kind of corners. Not friends. Not strangers. That dangerous middle that turns names into bullets.

Words carry weight. Some weigh a little; some hit the ground and crack. I couldn't hear theirs over the bass and the brag of the block, but I could read the conversation in shoulders: CJ's were relaxed until they weren't, Hoodie's were hungry. The boys behind him made a movie of the moment. An arm lifted. A chin tipped up. Posture became prophecy.

"Go," I said, low, not begging. "This ain't your part." CJ didn't answer me. He spoke two sentences to Hoodie I couldn't catch and lifted his palms the way men do when they're trying to show you they don't need their hands to win. It might have worked in a different story. Not this one.

I saw the gun before I heard it. You always do if you're looking the right way. No recollection of the first shot, but I remember ducks lifting off a puddle two blocks over like they'd gotten a memo. I remember the way the crowd opened without anyone deciding; people parting the way water does around a rock. I recall CJ's hand on my shoulder hard, push rather than touch, and then my door slammed and we were moving, tires loud, hearts louder.

He didn't burn out. He didn't flex it. He drove like a person who has counted every red light on a route and knows exactly where to breathe. My fingers had a mind of their own and folded into prayer without asking me first. I don't remember praying. I remember inventory: I am whole. He is whole. The car is intact. The rearview is full of tail-lights, not sirens. The world is still pretending this is a normal night.

"Look at me," he said after two blocks. I did. "You straight?"

"I'm straight," I lied, then swallowed and made it true.

We didn't go home. We went to a lot nobody was using, the kind with grass defiantly growing through cracks. He cut the engine. The night pressed its ear to the windows to listen. "You ain't gotta talk," he said, forearms on the wheel, forehead on forearms.

"I ain't got nothin' to say," I said, eyes on his knuckles, skin stretched over tendons like wire.

He exhaled through his nose, a small laugh that wasn't funny. "You always got somethin' to say," he said. "Just not to me right now."

I stared out at the halo of light around the one working streetlamp. "You told me to keep a piece back," I said. "I'm keeping it."

That made him turn. He studied my face like it was a map he wanted to buy. "Good," he said finally. "Keep it. You gon' need it."

I didn't ask for details. The streets deliver those free and unkind. By midnight, the story had a hundred versions and none of them mattered. Who disrespected who, who started it, who fired first, who hit what. What mattered was the math: bodies turn into cases; cases turn into heat; heat turns into time.

The knock came two mornings later, that polite-rude police rhythm you hear in movies and then hate for real. Two detectives, one who introduced himself and one who didn't. They smelled like stale coffee and the air-conditioned inside of a cruiser. Their eyes did that soft thing that's supposed to make you confess.

"We just wanna talk," the talker said. "We heard you were with Mr. Johnson that evening."

I lifted a shoulder. "I don't keep other people's calendars."

"You Jasmine Carter?" the quiet one asked, flipping open a little book like he was reading a magic spell off the page.

"Depends who asking," I said, and made my mouth into a line. Not cute. Not disrespectful. Just closed.

They tried angles. Good cop, good cop. They asked if I was safe. They asked if anybody had threatened me. They asked if I needed protection. Their language was a pile of careful furniture they hoped I would trip on.

"I'm good," I said every time. It was a blanket answer. I tucked it around my ankles and didn't let my toes show.

"You a smart girl," the talker said finally, tilting his head like we were cousins. "Smart girls don't get themselves buried for somebody else's mistakes."

I thought of my mama on the bathroom floor with the needle in the sink, of the midwife who caught me, of Laverne's kitchen and church mints and folded dollars and couch rules. I thought of the first slap that taught me silence is sometimes the only weapon you own.

"I'm a girl that got somewhere to be," I said. "Y'all done?" They left a card like a prayer card — flat, pointless, offered more for the giver than the receiver. I used it to level a crooked table leg.

The arrest felt inevitable, not shocking. CJ called me himself after they picked him up, voice steady like he'd practiced it. My throat went tight at the sound of the jail-house prelude, "This is a collect call from..."

"Listen, I'm gon' handle it. You ain't see nothin'. You ain't say nothin'. You don't let nobody scare you into talkin'."

"I know the rules," I said, small because the metal echo on the line made it hard to be big.

He didn't waste words on sorry. He never did. "You eat?"

I took a breath and let the question land. "Lemon pepper," I said, and he smiled into the phone - I could hear it.

"Aight," he said. "Keep your hat low. I'll call when I can."

The jail smelled like bleach and men's fear. The first time I went, a guard told me to spit out my gum like I was twelve, and I did it because you pick your battles when the floor belongs to somebody else. The plastic chair under me was bolted to the ground.

A woman three seats over cried into a receiver like the crying could travel through the glass and meet something on the other side. CJ came out in orange, eyes clear. He sat. He looked at me like he was checking for cracks.

"You good," he said, not asking.

"Always," I said. "You?"

He shrugged one shoulder — more expression than the guards probably liked. "Temporary," he said.

Temporary stretched into a calendar. Court dates have a way of erasing whole months with one postponement. I learned a new kind of waiting, the thin kind, stretched like a rubber band between hope and what I knew already.

The DA said words like premeditated and reckless disregard and prior incidents; those words piled up until they weighed more than one night in a parking lot. His lawyer wore a suit that fit but not like money. His mama sat two rows up with a tissue crushed in her hand so tight that when she let go, the tissue stayed shaped like fist. I bought a dress that looked like church and sat quiet, hands folded, hat left at home because the courthouse wanted faces uncovered.

When the verdict came, the courtroom did what rooms do; it kept being a room. The air didn't rush out. The judge didn't turn into a dragon. The ceiling didn't fall. Everybody just breathed in, kept that breath and looked at their own hands, as if theirs had pronounced his guilt.

The world didn't move. It sat down. CJ turned once and found me. I lifted my chin. No crying. Not now. He mouthed a sentence I pretended I couldn't read because reading it out loud in my head would break something I didn't have a replacement for.

After, outside, the sky had the nerve to be beautiful. Tika hugged me sideways and whispered, "You okay?" like it was a password.

"I'm hungry," I said, because hunger was the only true sentence left, and we went to get wings because grief doesn't cancel appetite. It makes it rude.

That night, I lay on a bed that wasn't mine and stared at a ceiling I hadn't named. The quiet was too loud. I pulled my hat down low, even though the dark doesn't need disguises, and told myself a story. This ain't the end. It's the beginning of the part where I learn how to breathe underwater.

CJ had filled me with rules. Don't show your whole love. Keep a piece. See it first. But my mama left me one, too: Don't trust no man. I put those together on the table like playing cards and made a house out of them. Then I blew on it, gentle, to see if it would stand. It didn't. Not yet.

The calls kept coming. He sent game through metal and wire like he was teaching class from a submarine. "Put money in this name." "Don't post nothin' that look like you braggin'." "Keep your circle little like a period." "If anybody ask you about me, tell 'em you praying."

"I don't pray," I said once, tired of words pretending to hold the building up.

"You do now," he said, not mean, just sure.

I tasted the word loyalty in my mouth like a coin. Heavy. Cold. Valuable but not food. I had to eat and I had to decide whether love was groceries or jewelry - consumable or display. The girls I halfway liked started booking video shoots, coming home with stories about green rooms and per diems and rappers who spent money like it was water. I watched. I wasn't scared of cameras. I was scared of belonging to them.

"You could do it," Tika said, filing her nails down to weapons. "You prettier than half them."

"Pretty don't keep you safe," I said.

"Neither do broke," she shot back, and we laughed like the joke wasn't standing on both our chests.

Even though I hardly came through anymore, on Sundays I still went to Laverne's, sat at the same table, let collards remind me there were greens that weren't money. "You carrying something heavy," she said without turning, tasting the air like grandmothers do.

"I always am," I said.

She clicked her tongue. "You ain't got to do it by yourself."

"I know," but I didn't put it down.

When I walked home alone, I noticed that my shadow had learned how to split. The hat took one piece; my quiet took another. I kept the last part, the one I didn't let CJ have, even when I wanted to hand him everything. That piece whispered different lessons than his. It said, "You can love someone and still choose you." "Sometimes the safest place is the one nobody knows you live." "Everything they taught you, learn it; everything they didn't teach you, invent."

The game's first lesson wasn't his, it was mine. I could be the girl in the passenger seat, I could be the driver, I could be the visible crown, I could be the invisible hand. The word for it had not yet come, not the name that would follow me into rooms like smoke. But I felt it growing under my skin, something thin and fast, something that knew how to move without leaving fingerprints.

When the phone rang late and the robotic woman said, "This is a collect call from..." I pressed one and listened to a voice belonging to a past that refused to stay put.

"You good?" he asked, first words always the same.

"Always," I said, and this time the lie didn't need help.

"I'm proud of you," with his voice unflinching.

"For what?"

"For seeing it," he said. "For staying quiet. For not needing me."

I didn't tell him I still did. I didn't tell him I didn't. I pressed my forehead to the wall and let the cool run into me like water.

After we hung up, I stood in front of a mirror nailed to the back of a door and tried on three different hats. Brim straight. Brim bent. Knit pulled low enough to make me someone else. I tilted my head. I watched my mouth change when I decided it needed to. I practiced the smile that closed negotiations. I practiced the stare that started them. I practiced being a rumor.

The streets outside kept their argument with the night. Somebody laughed like they didn't care who heard. A siren had a short conversation with a distant siren and then quit. I lay down and let the city talk to itself.

Morning would come. Money would need making. The world wouldn't slow down to count my feelings. And if love couldn't feed me, the game would. I pulled the brim down, just enough, and went to sleep already halfway gone.

CHAPTER

4

Life After the Gavel

The courthouse smelled like polish and old wood, like the whole place was trying too hard to cover up rot. After waiting so many weeks, when the word 'life' left the judge's mouth, I didn't cry. Couldn't. Tears felt like a luxury in a room full of people who wanted to see me break.

CJ turned once before they pulled him out. His lips moved. I refused to read them. I wasn't about to carry his last look into my sleep. He gave me rules, I kept them. He gave me promises, I believed some. Now he was behind a wall, and I was standing on a sidewalk watching people go on about their business, like the world hadn't just swallowed me whole yesterday.

My cousin asked if I was ok, her hand on my shoulder. I pulled away. "Always." It became my script.

Nights stretched longer after the sentencing. I'd lie on whatever couch or mattress I landed on, staring at ceilings I didn't choose, and feel the space CJ used to fill like a missing tooth.

At first the calls came: This is a collect call from— then his voice, steady. "You good?"

"Always."

"You stayin' focused?"

"Always."

But after I hung up, I was just a girl in the dark with no plan and a pocket of crumpled dollars. I realized quick that if I didn't step out his shadow, I was gonna die in it.

Without CJ, people looked at me different.

Girls tilted their heads: "What you gon' do now, Jas? Ain't no princess without a kingdom."

Boys leaned too close: "CJ gone. You don't gotta starve, baby. I can put you on."

I learned to end conversations with one look -chin high, eyes flat. But the whispers stayed. So I did what I always did. I hustled.

It started at Ms. Cheryl's beauty shop. I was sitting under a dryer flipping through an old magazine when she started complaining loud. "Got these new shops tryin' to steal my clients," she muttered, snatching bills from the register. "They out here passing flyers like candy. If I had somebody to run the block for me, I'd—"

"I can do it," I said before I thought.

Cheryl looked me up and down, eyebrow arched. "You? Girl, the streets gon' eat you alive."

I stared right back. "They already tried. I'm still here."

She smirked. "Smart mouth. Fine. Fifty dollars. You get every head that walk by here a flyer, you hear me? Don't be standin' there lookin' cute, either. You workin'."

"Bet," was my only response.

I walked the block until my feet burned, handing out papers, smiling the smile I practiced in mirrors. By evening, I had fifty in my pocket and another twenty Cheryl slipped me when she saw the chairs filling.

"You different," she said, stuffing rollers into a girl's hair. "Most little girls want handouts. You want hustle."

"I don't like owing nobody," I told her.

She pointed her comb at me like it was a sword. "Keep that. Owing folks worse than being broke."

That night I counted my money three times, just to feel it real. It wasn't much. But it was mine.

A week later, a photographer came by the shop dropping off headshots. His camera swung heavy on his chest, lens glinting. He stopped mid-sentence when he saw me.

"You ever model?" he asked. I shook my head.

"You should," he said, handing me a card. "Girls like you get paid to look at a camera the way you just looked at me."

Ms. Cheryl cut in quick. "Don't be tryna turn my shop into your scouting ground."

The man laughed, eyes still on me. "Just saying. If you ever want to try, call."

That night, I stood in front of the mirror with his card on the sink. Turned my face left, right. Smiled. Didn't smile. Lowered my hat brim, tilted my chin. Every angle told a different story.

For the first time, I wondered if survival could look like more than just scraping by. Maybe beauty wasn't just a shield. Maybe it was a weapon.

By fifteen, promoters started letting me in clubs for free. "Bring your pretty friends," they'd say, sliding wristbands like golden tickets.

Inside was another world: neon lights painting everybody the same shade of red and blue, smoke curling over bass lines, men with bottles flexing like trophies.

I wasn't drinking. I was watching.

I saw how fast money made women forget themselves. I saw how men turned soft words into hard hands when the night got too late. I saw how everybody wanted something, and almost nobody wanted to pay full price.

A promoter leaned close one night, breath hot in my ear. "You keep showing up, Jas, I'll make sure you always got a section."

I smiled without teeth. "I don't sit at tables I didn't pay for."

He laughed, trying to play it off. "Girl, you savage."

"Smart," I corrected, walking away.

By the end of the night, three rappers had sent drinks, two photographers asked for my number, and one chick tried to size me up like she wanted to fight. I went home without a scratch, without paying a dime, and with four new connections in my phone.

Walking home one night, Tika asked, "You think CJ gon' make it out? Appeal or somethin'?"

I pulled my jacket tighter. "CJ made his choices. Now I gotta make mine."

She frowned. "Damn, you cold."

"I'm alive," I said. And I meant it.

By sixteen, people stopped calling me CJ's girl and started calling me Jas the Hustler. I liked the sound of it better.

I wasn't running wild — not yet — but I was moving smart. Making money off looks, off charm, off being invisible when I wanted and unforgettable when I needed.

Every time I pulled a brim low or tilted my face just right, I felt that shadow-self grow stronger. A mask. A version of me nobody could touch. The word wasn't there yet. But the idea was.

Phantum.

CHAPTER 5

Becoming Phantum

The first time I cut my hair short, it wasn't about style. It was about power.

I stood in front of the cracked bathroom mirror with clippers borrowed from Tika's cousin, the hum loud in my chest. My curls dropped in little black piles on the tile, soft as dust. Every swipe took another piece of the old me away.

"You crazy as hell," Tika said, leaning in the doorway, chewing on a Now & Later. "CJ gon' lose his damn mind if he see you like that."

I looked her dead in the face through the mirror. "CJ don't see me. And I ain't his no more."

She sucked her teeth. "Mmm. You tryna reinvent yourself or some shit?"

"Damn right."

When I leaned back, my face stared at me raw, uncovered. It was like meeting myself for the first time. The girl who used to hide behind hair and hats was gone.

The next day, I bought a box of blonde dye from the corner store. Cheap brand, strong enough to peel paint. I sat in the bathroom while the chemicals burned my scalp, teeth clenched, eyes watering.

"You sure about this?" Tika asked, wrinkling her nose at the smell.

"Shut the fuck up," I hissed, gripping the edge of the sink. "It's supposed to hurt."

When I rinsed it out, a stranger looked back at me — sharp, bold, loud. That was the night I whispered to myself for the first time: Phantum.

Not Jasmine. Not CJ's little queen. Not nobody's baby. Phantum. A name for the version of me you'd never see coming.

A week later, I was cleaning out one of CJ's old spots, a ragged little apartment on the Southside where he used to lay low. Most of his shit was gone, but something told me to check the baseboards.

Sure enough, one was loose. I pried it open and there it was: a dusty shoebox.

I flipped the lid, and my heart almost stopped. Stacks. Not cartel money, but more cash than I'd ever touched at once. Rubber bands tight, faces staring up at me like they'd been waiting.

"Holy shit," Tika gasped, eyes wide. "Girl, we rich!"

I snapped the lid shut. "No. We funded."

For the first time in my life, I moved like I had options. I bought clothes — dresses that hugged my hips, jeans that made me feel taller, shoes that clicked sharp on concrete. I bought lip gloss that shimmered under club lights. I even paid for a hotel room one weekend just to stretch out on clean white sheets without hearing somebody else's kids crying through the wall.

Me and Tika went shopping downtown, bags swinging from both arms. "This what the fuck I'm talking about," Tika laughed, spinning in a pair of new heels. "We up, bitch!"

I grinned but kept it measured. "We temporarily up. Don't get comfortable."

Tika rolled her eyes. "Why you always gotta ruin the moment? Damn, enjoy it."

I did. But in the back of my mind, I was already counting. And money runs like water if you don't know how to dam it.

Two months later, the shoebox was dust. All that was left were receipts, outfits I'd already worn twice, and a pair of sneakers I didn't even like anymore.

I sat on the bed one night with the empty box in my lap, head in my hands. "Fuck," I whispered.

Tika walked in, chomping on chips. "What's wrong with you?"

"It's gone," I muttered. "All of it."

She raised an eyebrow. "You shocked? Bitch, we been eatin' like rappers for weeks. You bought a whole hotel room just to watch cable."

I glared. "Don't act like you ain't been living off me too."

She laughed, unbothered. "True. But you the one played rich. Lesson learned, huh?"

"Yeah." I sighed. "Lesson learned."

But deep down, I knew the hunger was louder now. Because once you taste full, empty feels like hell.

That's when another photographer came back around. Hustler type, camera swinging from his neck like jewelry. He saw me at Cheryl's shop, blonde hair catching the light.

"Damn," he muttered, snapping his fingers. "That look suits you. You ever model?"

I smirked. "Everybody keeps askin' me that."

He slid a card into my hand. "Come by the studio. No bullshit. I'll shoot you for free the first time. You got...something."

Tika leaned over my shoulder as he walked out. "Girl, he tryna smash."

"Maybe," I said, pocketing the card. "But he still got a camera. Cameras equal opportunity."

The shoot was awkward at first. Lights too bright, his voice telling me to pose this way, turn that way. But when I saw the photos — me, blonde cut sharp, lips glossy, eyes cutting straight through the lens — I almost didn't recognize myself.

"That's not Jasmine," I whispered, scrolling through the screen. "That's somebody else."

"That's Phantum," the photographer grinned. And I didn't correct him.

With blonde hair and new pictures floating around, clubs started calling me instead of me begging at the door. Every night out, every photoshoot, every hustle taught me something.

Blonde hair made me unrecognizable to people who once called me CJ's girl.
A tilted hat made me invisible in rooms where I didn't need to be seen.A smile at the right

moment made doors open that would've stayed locked.

I was Jasmine in the birth certificate, Jas to the ones who thought they knew me, but under the lights, behind the mask, moving fast and quiet, I was Phantum. And Phantum didn't just survive. She planned. She plotted. She ate.

CHAPTER

6

Fame in the Flash

The first time I saw my face on glossy paper,
I almost dropped it.

It was 'Straight Stuntin', behind the counter
at the corner store. I flipped it open just to pass
time, and there I was — blonde cut, legs out,
lips slick with gloss.

"Daaaamn," Tika gasped, grabbing at the
rack of beauty mags. "That's you?! Centerfold
ass bitch! You famous now."

I yanked it back before her greasy fingers
smudged it. "Don't touch my face, girl. That's
money right there."

She laughed so hard people in the aisle
turned to look. "Look at you, actin' brand new.
Miss Magazine!" I smiled, but inside? My chest
thumped heavy. Jasmine from Capitol Homes

— who once cried over ketchup sandwiches —
now staring back at herself like a dream.

But it wasn't a dream. It was the start.

The mansion looked rich, but up close it
smelled like sweat, weed, and cheap
champagne. Ten models crowded the place,
heels too high, attitudes higher.

The director, short with a hat turned
backwards, barked: "Yo, blondie, poolside. Give
me fire. Don't look thirsty." As I walked by, one
girl with a red weave rolled her eyes so hard I
thought they'd fall out.

"She only here 'cause she blonde," she
muttered loud enough for the room. "Bitch
look like a knockoff Amber Rose."

I stopped, turned slow, and smiled. "Funny,
last time I checked, they don't book knockoffs.
Guess that makes you background." The other
girls laughed. Red went quiet, lips tight.

"Yo, less talking, more posing!" the director
snapped. I slid my shades down, smirked, and
strutted to the pool. My body talked louder
than words — hips slow, eyes sharp, lips
parting just right.

When the music cut, the rapper himself
came over, blunt in hand. "Yo, who shorty?" he
asked his manager.

"That's Phantum," the man said.

The rapper squinted at me. "Why they call you that?"

I tilted my head. "'Cause you'll never see me coming...but you'll feel me when I leave." His whole crew hollered. The girls' faces twisted up tighter than wigs under sweat.

Friday night at Onyx, the line stretched around the block. The promoter spotted me and lit up. "Phantum! In the flesh. Come on, bring your crew."

Inside, the club was alive — smoke wafting, bass punching, money raining. We slid into VIP, promoters waving like proud uncles. A rapper shoved a bottle in my hand. "Drink up, blondie."

I smiled, pretended to sip, then set it down. "I don't drink brown."

He leaned in, grinning. "So what you drink?"

"Whatever pays my rent." His boys howled. He blinked like he wasn't sure if I was joking. That was the trick.

Later that night, another promoter leaned against me. "Yo, you keep pulling like this, I'll get you your own section."

I leaned back. "Sections ain't free. You got rent money with that offer?" His mouth opened, then closed. Tika snorted behind me. I walked away before he caught his breath.

The prison phone rang the next week. "This is a collect call from..." CJ's voice cut in, steady. "You good?" he asked.

"Always."

"You stayin' out the bullshit?"

"Depends what you call bullshit."

"Don't play with me, Jas," his voice dropped. "I know how this city move. I heard you in videos now, magazines, clubs every night. Don't let these clown-ass niggas turn you into a puppet."

I laughed sharp. "Puppet? CJ, I'm the one pulling strings now."

Silence. Then: "Don't forget who gave you the game."

"You gave me rules," I snapped. "But I'm the one living them. I'm out here flipping connections into condos, into cars. That ain't you — that's me."

He breathed heavy through the receiver. "Watch your mouth."

"Why?" I leaned close to the phone, eyes cold. "You locked down. You don't get to control me anymore."

He went quiet, then said low: "Just... don't let the streets chew you up, Jas. You worth more."

I swallowed. For a moment, Jasmine wanted to cry. But Phantum? She only said: "I know."

At another photoshoot, Red Weave circled back, her voice sharp. "You hot now, but shit can change for you real soon. Bet they drop you in six months."

I didn't even blink. "Maybe. But by then I'll own what I need. You'll still be beggin' for exposure." Her face cracked.

Another girl whispered, "Damn, she cuttin' throats out here."

I smiled. "Nah. Just speaking facts."

Later, at a party, a rapper's wife pulled me aside, nails digging into my arm. "Don't get comfortable, little girl. Men like him don't save bitches like you. They use you. They throw you away."

I smiled sweet. "Then maybe I'll use him first."

Her eyes went wide. She slapped the drink out my hand, liquid splashing down my dress. The room froze.

I didn't flinch. I leaned in, whispered in her ear: "You think you the only one with claws?

Try me again." Then I walked off, head high, leaving whispers swirling.

By seventeen, Jasmine didn't exist anymore. Jasmine was the girl who begged for cornbread, who cried over her mama's body, who waited for CJ to call.

Phantum was the woman who walked into a club and owned the air. She flipped rappers into rent, athletes into cars, promoters into pawns.

Sitting in my condo one night, Tika sprawled on my couch eating wings, she said, "Bitch, you really out here like a ghost. Poppin' up, disappearing, gettin' what you want, then gone."

I smirked. "That's why they call me Phantum." At first it was just a tagline, but now I was living it — because they never did see me coming, and they always felt me when I left.

Onyx was packed wall to wall that Friday. Lights strobing, smoke thick, bass so loud the air shook in your chest. Tika and me strutted into VIP like we owned it because at that point, we basically did.

I leaned back, legs crossed, blonde cut catching every flash of the lights. Bottles popped, sparklers fizzed, and I let the city watch me without lifting a finger.

That's when I saw her. Red Weave. Same
girl from the photo shoot. Titties bouncing,
sashaying into our section with two other girls,
laughing too loud. She caught my eye and
smirked.

"Look who it is," she said, loud enough for
the music break to carry it. "Miss Phantum.
Thought you'd be too busy tryna be famous to
hang with the regulars."

Her friends cackled. The promoter's eyes
darted between us, nervous. I sipped my water
slow, then smiled. "Sweetheart, you call
yourself a regular? That explains why nobody
remembers your name."

The section oooh'd like a middle-school
fight. Red's face tightened, lips curling. "Bitch,
don't get cute. You really think you the shit. Fat
asses come a dime a dozen."

"Maybe," I said, setting my glass down. "But
at least when I walk in, I don't disappear into
the wallpaper."

The crowd laughed, but Red wasn't done.
She stepped closer, voice sharp. "You think
these niggas love you? You just another face in
rotation. They gon' fuck you, forget you, and
move on."

The music dipped right then, like the DJ
himself wanted to hear what I'd say.

I leaned forward, my voice clear enough to cut through the beat. "Difference between me and you? When they done with you, you go home with nothing. When they done with me... I'm driving a Lexus to a condo with my name on the lease."

The whole VIP section erupted. Even a couple rappers started hollering, "Daaamn!" and clapping.

Red froze. Her girls tugged her arm, trying to pull her back, but the damage was done.

I stood, smoothed my dress, and looked around the section — promoters, rappers, bottle girls, all eyes on me. "I ain't here to be loved," I said, voice steady. "I'm here to be remembered. And whether you hate me or not... you will."

I grabbed Tika's hand, stepped down from VIP, and walked straight out of the club. Heads turned as we passed, phones up, whispers chasing us like shadows.

By the time the night ended, Atlanta had a new story to tell. And it was mine.

CHAPTER 7

Model Dreams, Street Reality

That first 'Straight Stuntin' spread was cool, but it was just the beginning. The real calls started after that — Black Men. Smooth.

The bigger shoots meant more eyes, more photographers, and more mouths talking about me.

By then, my body had caught up with my name. My booty sat phatter than it did a year ago, thighs hugging tighter from me working out in the mornings, and my skin glowed like cocoa dipped in honey. Walking into a room, I could feel eyes stick to me like tape.

"Damn, you seen Phantum lately? That ass sittin' different." "Bruh, them thighs look like they could crack a rib." "She the baddest in Atlanta right now. No cap."

Even the haters couldn't deny it. They just dressed their jealousy in shade.

The studio lights were blinding, cameras clicking like gunfire. I stepped out in a red bikini, heels making my legs look endless. My thighs, tight from squats, caught the light just right, booty round and firm as I arched my back.

"Perfect, baby, perfect!" the photographer shouted, sweat dripping as he circled with the camera.

Behind him, one of the assistants muttered under his breath, "God damn, shorty built like a stallion."

The other nodded. "That's cover material right there."

I smirked, moving slow, milking the angles.

But during the break, the head photographer leaned close, voice low. "You know... I could get you more covers. All you gotta do is let me spend some time with you... off the clock."

I stared at him, smile never slipping. "Funny. I thought my ass already got me covers. Not yours." He chuckled nervously, backing off. But I knew he'd try again — they always did.

The 'Smooth' shoot was next-level. Fancy studio, racks of designer clothes. I slipped into a gold one-piece that hugged every curve, thighs gleaming under the lights. Girls across the room whispered, rolling eyes so hard they almost fell out.

"Look at her. Acting like she invented ass."

I smiled to myself. Because jealousy was louder when the truth was undeniable.

On set, I laid back across velvet, skin glowing, body talking in every shot. The photographer's hands shook on the camera. "Yes, yes! That's the money shot!"

When the magazine dropped, my spread was centerfold. The same girls were background blur, their shade buried in silence.

That week, Tika came home laughing. "Girl, you know you famous when niggas in the barbershop talk about you like sports stats. They in there arguing like, 'Phantum the baddest in the game right now. Ain't nobody touching her.' One dude said your ass 'look like it came with surround sound.'"

I burst out laughing. "Not surround sound!"

"Facts," Tika said, grinning. "Even the old heads talking about you. And the girls? Whew. They salty."

For all the love, the reality was still grimy.

The last photographer was now blowing up my phone, offering "private sessions." A promoter promised me three hundred for a club walk-in, then tried to slide me fifty and a bottle of cheap champagne.

I shoved the bottle back in his chest. "Nigga, fifty dollars don't get me out of bed. Try again." He stammered, red-faced. His crew laughed at him. Another story to my legend.

But still, checks came late. Contracts were trash. Fame looked sweet, but I learned quick it was just sugar on top of dirt.

Back at the condo, Tika sprawled on the couch, flipping through Smooth with me centerfolded. "Look at this shit, Jas. You really made it."

I shook my head. "Nah. I ain't made it till I can stop countin' bills twice to make sure rent clear."

She raised her brow. "You got the face, the ass, the whole city watching. That's currency."

I smirked. "Exactly. And I'm cashin' it in."
Because the model dream was cute. But the
street reality? That's where survival lived.

CHAPTER

8

Double Lives

By the time my third spread dropped, I wasn't just "that blonde chick from a magazine." I was the one promoters, athletes, and rappers was begging for.

But here's what they ain't know: the magazine shit was just the dream. The hustle was still the reality. And that's where the double life kicked in.

A promoter had been on my line for weeks. "Yo, lemme take you out. You too fine to be out here worryin' about little shit. I'm the one who can upgrade you."

Usually, I curved niggas like that. But something in his voice screamed "lick." Too eager. Too flashy. Too desperate to prove he had money.

So I said yes.

We met at a Buckhead lounge — candles lit, soft music, waiters dressed like they was auditioning for a movie. He walked in loud as hell, chain swinging, watch catching the lights. Talking on his phone like three people cared.

"Yeah, yeah, tell shorty it's on me, I cover the whole thing. I got bread like that." He snapped his fingers at me like I was supposed to be impressed.

I sat there in a silk dress, sipping my drink, letting him think he was running shit.

When he finally sat down, he grinned wide. "God damn, Phantum in the flesh. You look even better than the magazines. Niggas ain't lying."

I tilted my head, smirked. "Magazines don't do me justice."

He laughed. "You got a mouth on you. I like that. But real talk, you don't gotta hustle no more. You get with me, you set. Condo, car, the works."

I leaned forward, chin resting on my hand. "Mmm. You talk nice. But talk cheap. Where the keys at?"

He chuckled, tapping his watch against the table. "Baby, this Rolex worth more than your rent."

I smiled sweet, never breaking eye contact. "Cute flex. But my landlord don't take watches."

The waiter slid up. He waved him off. "Get us the best bottle you got, don't even tell the price." I bit back a laugh. Niggas love flexin' with other people watching.

Halfway through the meal, he excused himself to the bathroom, probably to stare in the mirror and practice his smile. I pulled my phone out under the table, screen dimmed low.

Yo. Candy ripe. Flashy as fuck. Buckhead spot. Pull up 20 after. Lot sweet.

Three dots. Then a reply: Say no more.

I slid my phone back into my clutch, took another sip of wine, and put my sweetest smile on when he came back.

He sat down, napkin back in his lap, grinning. "Man, when I put you in that condo, you gon' forget all these little niggas chasing you."

I laughed soft. "You gon' put me in a condo? What, tomorrow?"

"Tonight if you want."

"Then slide me the lease, baby," I said, licking cheesecake off the fork. "Keys don't come with promises. They come with paperwork."

He laughed so hard he slapped the table. "You dangerous. I like that."

I leaned in, lowering my voice like a secret. "Dangerous is my middle name." He thought I was flirting. Really, I was just telling the truth.

When the bill came, he made a whole show, throwing down hundreds like he was in a movie. "Keep the change," he told the waiter loud. I smiled sweet. Inside, I was rolling my eyes.

"Walk me to my car?" I asked, voice soft.

"Of course, baby."

We strolled into the lot, his chain swinging like bait on a hook. I slipped my phone from my clutch, pressed the flashlight on, then off. The signal.

They came out the shadows quick — two hoodies, gloves, faces masked. "Yo, what the fuck?!" he shouted as one slammed him against his car.

"Run it fuck nigga," one of them barked.

Face shocked as death looked him in the eye, he twisted and yelled, "Nah, nah, this some bullshit!" But the second one already had his chain in his hand, Rolex yanked clean, wallet snatched.

I screamed like it was the end of the world. "Oh my God! Please, don't hurt him! Just take it and go!"

One of the masked men shoved him again and slapped him with the pistol for show, then they vanished into the night like smoke.

The Sucka stumbled back, face red, breathing heavy. "What the fuck just happened?!"

I ran to him, putting on the best performance of my life, clutching his arm. "Oh my God, baby, I was so scared! They came outta nowhere! Are you okay?!"

He looked at me wild-eyed. "They ain't touch you. Not once. You…"

"I was screaming!" I cut in, letting my voice shake. "I thought they was gon' kill us! Why you even wearing all that shit out here?!"

He blinked, confused, trying to piece it together. But I didn't let him. I kept my eyes wide, my breath fast, my act flawless.

He kicked the tire of his car, cussing under his breath. "This city fucked up, man." Inside, my heart was pounding, pussy was thumping. Not from fear. From the thrill of it all.

I pulled up to my building, slid in the car where Tika was waiting. She was already grinning, eyes on the bag of cash in my hand. "Bitch, you deserve a damn award," she laughed. "Girl, you screamed like somebody was murdering you. I almost believed that shit."

I shot her a look. "That's the point. He'll never question me. If he talk about it, all he can say is we got robbed. And I was the scared little model screaming in the corner."

Tika shook her head, laughing. "Cold-blooded."

I lit a cigarette, blowing smoke out slow. "Smart."

Then she did it — dropped the name I hated. "You know...CJ would've been proud seeing that. That was some straight CJ shit."

My face snapped toward her. "Don't say his fucking name."

She blinked. "Damn, chill. I'm just saying, he taught you how to think like this."

My voice rose. "He ain't here, Ti! He don't get no credit for this! I'm the one out here risking my neck, playing both sides. Don't shrink me down into his shadow."

She frowned, voice soft. "You sound bitter."

I tapped the wheel hard, eyes on the road. "I sound free. Stop bringing him up, or next time we riding alone."

The car went silent, tension heavy. But me? I was buzzing inside. Not from fear. Not from guilt. From the high. Being Phantum meant living two lives. And I wasn't about to give either one up.

Next day I pulled up to the studio like nothing happened. Hair laid, skin glowing like cocoa butter in sunlight, ass sittin' fat in the dress the stylist pulled.

The photographer's eyes lit up soon as I walked in. "Phantum! That's my girl! We gon' make magic today." I slid in the chair, makeup brush sweeping across my cheek, when I caught the whispers behind me.
Two bitches huddled in the corner, thinkin' they slick. "I heard shorty lined a nigga up last night."

"Swear to God, that's what they say. She model by day, scammer by night." "She dangerous as fuck. That's why dudes so pressed on her."

I smirked at my reflection, tongue running across my teeth. "Y'all hoes whispering like I'm deaf." My voice cut the room in half. "If you gon' talk about me, be woman enough to say that shit *to me*."

They froze. One looked at the floor, the other fumbled with her phone.

I laughed low, mean. "Yeah, that's what the fuck I thought. Keep my name out y'all dick-sucking mouths unless you ready to put some respect on it."

The makeup girl damn near dropped her brush. Whole room quiet. Then the photographer clapped his hands loud. "Aight, let's roll, baby!"

I stood, heels clicking, slid on the lingerie like it was armor. Camera started flashing. I arched my back, lips parted, eyes locked on the lens like I owned it.

Perfect. Beautiful. Untouchable.

But inside? My blood was still buzzing. Not from fear. From the rush. The setup, the money, the whispers — all of it. And if they wanted to talk? Let 'em.

Legends don't get built off truth; legends get built off *rumors*.

CHAPTER

9

Social Media Fame

When Instagram first started buzzin', I ain't think too much of it. Just another app, right? Somewhere to drop a picture, maybe flex a lil'. But the first week I posted, shit went crazy.

Niggas I hadn't talked to since middle school slidin' in my comments like, "Yo, Jas, you fine as hell now." Girls I ain't never fucked with suddenly hittin' me up like, "Sis, you killin' it." I scrolled slow, tryna act like it ain't mean nothin', but I couldn't lie — it felt good.

Tika was next to me, legs crisscross on the couch, chompin' gum loud as hell. She snatched the phone out my hand before I could lock it.

"Bitch!" she shouted, eyes wide. "You see this shit? Two hundred likes in twenty minutes.

Two fuckin' hundred. Hoes be postin' all day tryna scrape up ten likes and you breakin' phones."

I reached for it, rolling my eyes. "It's just a picture."

She pulled back, laughing. "Nah, nah. Don't even play yourself like that. You know what you did with that angle. That ass pokin', waist snatched, face sittin' pretty. You dangerous on this app."

I smirked but kept it cool. "Man, stop hypin' me up."

She kept scrollin', gigglin'. "Look at these DMs though. Niggas thirsty as hell. Look..." She shoved the screen in my face.

Some dude with a rapper name I ain't recognize: "Let me fly you out, baby girl. I'll put you in a penthouse tonight."

Another: "You wife material, deadass. Where you from? You too bad to be local." And then: "Drop ya PayPal, I got you."

Tika fell back laughin', kickin' her legs. "Girl, you better get you a baller! Look at this dumb nigga tryna send money just 'cause you posted a selfie. You sittin' on a goldmine."

I snatched the phone back, scrolling quick, cheeks hot even though I fronted like it ain't faze me. "Half these niggas cappin'. They don't really mean that shit."

Tika sucked her teeth. "Cappin' or not, they tryna spend. That's the point. And you know what? You could play this whole app like a hustle. No gun, no risk. Just looks. You too fine not to eat off this."

I ain't say nothin', but in my chest, I felt it — she was right. IG wasn't just a game. It was a new block. And I was already the baddest bitch on the corner.

The more my page blew up, the more I felt it. I was living two damn lives.

Online? I looked like money. Glossy pics, filters hittin' just right, thighs sittin' fat, waist pulled tight. I dropped captions like they was scripture:

"Pretty but petty."

"Smile soft, heart cold."

"Queens move in silence."

And motherfuckers ate it up.

But offline? I was still Phantum. Still the bitch who could smile in your face and have your pockets tapped before you made it back home. Still movin' like a ghost in the night.

Tika sprawled out on my bed one night, her cracked phone glowing in her hand. She scrolled slow, shaking her head. "Look at these dumbass niggas in your comments. 'Wifey material,' 'I'll drink your bath water,' 'Queen energy.' Girl, they think you soft as fuck."

I laughed, a sharp sound. "Soft? Shit. These niggas don't know I'll line they ass up soon as they blink."

Tika cracked up, kicking her feet. "That's the crazy part. Online, you sweet as honey. Real life? You the devil in Dior. They don't even see it."

I smirked, watching the glow from her screen reflect off the gold bracelet CJ once gave me. "That's the game. Keep 'em guessing. They can't touch what they can't figure out."

Tika nodded like she was proud. "Two different Jas's. Insta-Jas and Phantum-Jas. Good girl, bad girl. You playin' both masks better than anybody I know."

I leaned back, grinning slow. "And the best part? Both of 'em real."

Late at night, I'd scroll my own page, studying the comments. Niggas fighting each other in my mentions, girls droppin' heart emojis, people I ain't even met calling me #Goals.

They wasn't looking at me. They was looking at the illusion I fed them. And that shit? That was power.

It was late when Aunt Laverne knocked on my door. She never knocked.

Her face looked older than I remembered, lines deep, eyes red. She sat down heavy on the edge of my bed like the world had climbed on her back.

"Jas..." her voice cracked. "Baby, I got somethin' to tell you."

My stomach flipped. "What?"

She pressed her lips tight before the words came out. "It's Keekee. She gone."

The room spun.

I blinked at her, thinking I heard wrong. "Gone? What you mean, gone?"

"She dead." Laverne's voice broke, tears welling up in her tired eyes. "They said it happened quick. Some street shit. I don't know all the details. I just...I just know she ain't comin' back."

My chest tightened so hard I couldn't breathe. I felt heat rush up my neck, but my body was ice.

Keekee.

My big sister.

The same one who abandoned me, abandoned her baby. The same one I swore I hated for walking out.

And still — that was my blood.

I shook my head slow. "Nah...nah, you lyin'. Keekee ain't dead. She just out there, wildin' like always."

Aunt Laverne reached for my hand, but I pulled back. "Baby, the streets talkin'. Folks whisperin'...sayin' it was over some man, some drama she couldn't shake. Nobody sayin' names yet. Nobody givin' me straight answers. But Keekee gone, Jas. She gone."

Her words sliced through me, deep and cold. I stared at the wall, jaw locked, fists clenched till my nails dug into my palms.

I wanted to cry, but no tears came. Just this hard knot in my chest, like my whole childhood had finally been ripped away.

Keekee wasn't shit in a lot of ways. But she was mine. My sister. My first heartbreak and my first teacher in how cruel this world could be. And now she was a ghost.

That night I sat up scrolling through my phone, staring at old pictures. Keekee laughing, flipping her hair, holding her baby like she halfway cared. I remembered her voice bragging about Chris, about how he was gonna put her on.

The streets said she was dead over some man. I told myself I didn't care who it was. Told myself she left us long before death came for her. But deep down, I knew better. Deep down, I was already waiting to hear his name.

When Aunt Laverne told me Keekee was gone, I ain't shed one tear. Not a single fuckin' drop. I sat on the edge of my bed that night, staring at the wall, the baby picture of Keekee's little girl sitting on the dresser. My niece. Abandoned, just like me.

I thought about all them nights Keekee left me holding that baby while she chased after Chris. All the times she laughed in my face like I was too young to understand. All the times I swore I hated her for leaving us behind.

And now she was gone.

No warning. No goodbye. No second chance to fix it. Just...gone.

The streets was buzzing, but ain't nobody saying details. Just whispers. "Over some nigga drama." "She got caught slippin'." "Wrong place, wrong time."

My chest burned, but not from grief. From anger. Anger that she left her baby. Anger that she left me. Anger that the streets always swallowed the ones who thought they was too pretty, too slick to get caught.

But the thing that scared me most? The silence inside me. No scream. No tears. Just a cold, empty hole. So I did what I knew how to do — I buried that shit.

Instagram became my drug. Every like was a sip of numbness. Every DM was a hit that kept the pain out. Every fire emoji, every crown emoji, every thirsty comment, it was anesthesia.

I'd scroll through my feed for hours, posting pics back-to-back like my life depended on it. Smiling when I didn't feel like smiling. Posing like the world was mine when deep down, I felt hollow.

Tika noticed. She leaned over one night while we sat in my room. "You been postin' like crazy. You good?"

I shrugged, tapping my screen. "I'm straight."

"You don't even talk about Keekee no more," she pressed. "Like you don't even care."

My eyes snapped to hers. "Don't fuckin' say that. Don't you dare say that."

She held her hands up quick. "Aight, damn. I ain't mean it like that. I just...I know you. You hurtin'. You just won't let nobody see it."

I turned back to my phone, thumb scrolling. Notifications popping up nonstop. Heart emojis, DMs, tags.

"Let 'em see what I show 'em," I muttered. Because that was the truth. Online, I could be whoever the fuck I wanted. Beautiful. Untouchable. Unbothered.

Nobody had to know I was really just a broken girl who lost her sister and didn't even know how to cry about it.

Every post was a mask. And the more I posted, the less I felt. That's how I survived.

It started with a DM.

At first I thought it was just another thirsty nigga tryna shoot his shot. Username looked like some club name, page full of flyers. I almost ignored it.

But then I read it: "Yo Phantum, you fire. We got a spot this Friday, need some pretty faces to pull up. We'll pay you to host, drinks on us. All you gotta do is tag the club in your story."

I stared at the screen. Pay me? To show up?

Tika leaned over, snatching the phone, her eyes lighting up. "Bitch! They talkin' money! Look at this—five hundred just to sit in a VIP and sip on free liquor? You'd be crazy not to do it!"

I raised an eyebrow, half-skeptical. "So I just show up, post a lil' story, and leave with a bag? Sounds like bullshit."

Tika smirked. "Welcome to the new hustle, ho. This Instagram shit different. You a walking billboard now."

I thought about it all night. Money just to look good? Money for the same shit I already doin'?

When Friday came, I slid into a bodycon dress, heels clicking, mask on tight. The promoter met me at the door, grinning like he just booked Beyoncé.

"Damn, you even finer in person," he said, pressing a stack into my hand before I even made it inside. "All I need is one post. Show the world you here."

I nodded, sliding my phone out like it was second nature. Snap. Flash. Caption: "Outside tonight. Good vibes only. #Phantum"

Within minutes, my DMs flooded. Niggas asking what club. Girls asking where I got my dress. Comments blowing up like fireworks.

And me? I was five hundred richer, sipping on champagne I didn't pay for. That night I realized Instagram wasn't just attention. It was a weapon. A business. A hustle.

The streets gave me game. But Instagram? Instagram was giving me power.

CHAPTER

10

Tricks & Celebrities

The first time I saw a blue check slide into my DMs, I damn near dropped my phone. It wasn't just some random thirsty nigga anymore. This was different. This was status.

Tika was sprawled on the couch, eating Hot Cheetos, when I shoved the phone in her face. "Look at this shit."

She squinted, orange powder on her fingertips. "Hold up... bitch, is that who I think it is? That's that rapper nigga with the song all over YouTube!"

I smirked, leaning back. "Mhm. He said, 'Damn ma, you fire. I'ma be in Atlanta this weekend. Let's link.'"

Tika's jaw dropped. "He got, like, three million followers. Jas, that's a fuckin' blue check! Girl, you famous famous now."

I shrugged like it was nothing, but inside? My chest was lit. "It's just a DM."

She slapped my arm. "Just a DM? Ho, stop playin' humble. Niggas with blue checks don't slide in regular. They don't risk lookin' thirsty unless they want you bad."

I unlocked the screen again. And it wasn't just him. A couple ball players. A comedian. Even some actor from a movie. My inbox looked like a VIP guest list.

Scrolling through, Tika read them out loud, putting on voices like she was acting. "'Yo, queen, let me take care of you.'" "'Send me a pic just for me, I won't show nobody.'" "'Drop the PayPal, I'll make it worth your time.'"

She burst out laughing. "They sound desperate as hell! But desperate with money, and that's the best kinda desperate."

I gave her a side-eye, smirking. "They not the only ones desperate. Half these niggas already got girls at home."

Tika grinned wicked. "So? That ain't your problem. That's they problem. You ain't the one cheatin', you just collectin'."

I sat there quiet, scrolling, letting her words sink in. My phone buzzed again. Another blue check. Another opportunity.

It hit me then: this wasn't just IG clout. This was access. This was leverage. I could play these niggas like cards. And if I played it right, every hand was a winning one.

When I finally agreed to meet one of 'em, it was the rapper with the YouTube hit. His DM was simple: "Slide thru. Section on me." So I slid.

The club was packed, music thumping like it was shaking the walls. Soon as I walked in, I spotted him. He was easy to find — rappers always are. Brightest chain in the room, biggest crowd, loudest laugh.

But what caught my eye wasn't him. It was his setup. Two big-ass bodyguards, both built like brick walls, standing behind the velvet rope. One kept scanning the crowd, eyes cold. The other stayed glued to his phone but didn't move an inch. They wasn't just decoration; they was his shield.

Still, when he saw me, he broke into a grin like I was the only person in the room. "Yo! Phantum!" he shouted, arms wide. "Finally!"

He pulled me into the section, handing me a glass of champagne before I could even sit down. Bottles lined the table like soldiers, half-empty, gold labels shining.

He looked like money — diamond chain heavy, watch blinding, rings on every other finger. But under the lights, I could see it in his eyes: bloodshot, jittery. Dude was buzzing off more than liquor.

It didn't take long to see the real him.

One of his boys slid a tray across the table slick, like it was part of the show. White lines laid out neat as rails. He bent down quick, sniffed hard, came up smirking with powder on his nose.

I kept my face still, sipping my drink, but in my head I was taking notes. His hands trembled a little when he reached for his glass. His laugh came too loud, too sharp. Every few minutes, he leaned back and wiped his nose, then tossed another wad of cash in the air like it grew on trees.

"Yo, we spent fifty racks tonight already," he bragged, voice hoarse. "And I don't even feel it."

I smiled, leaning in close. "You don't even notice it gone, huh?"

He grinned, pupils wide. "Hell nah. Money always come back. I spend it, it come back triple. That's the game, baby."

But the way he said it? That wasn't confidence. That was delusion.

I watched him all night, watched how he moved. How the bodyguards kept people back but let him fall apart in plain sight. How he threw money to impress the crowd but forgot who was actually watching.

By the time the night ended, I knew what he was. Not a god. Not a superstar...

A sweet target. Drug habit. Loose lips. Too much pride.

And way too much money.

I left the club with his number in my phone, a designer bag on my arm, and the knowledge that he was already mine to play. Because a man that sloppy? He'd always pay to keep up the image.

And me? I was already plotting how to make him bleed slow. He thought linking with me was his jackpot.

Truth was, he was mine.

Every week it was the same routine — late-night calls, the Rolls Royce pulling up slick, him all coked out and grinning like he just won a prize. "Yo, Jas, come ride with me. Just me and you, baby."

I'd slide in the back seat, legs crossed, perfume heavy, eyes low. He always thought that was the night he'd finally fuck.

But nah.

See, coke had him fucked up. He was packing, no lie — dick big — but it never worked. He'd get hype, talking nasty, begging, but when it came time? Shit stayed soft as Play-Doh.

So I flipped the script.

"Boy, you talkin' too much," I'd whisper, pushing his head down. "You want me? Show me."

And he did. Every time. Eating pussy in the back of that Rolls like his life depended on it, thinking one day he'd finally hit.

But he never did. What he did do? Spend.

Week after week, bags landed in my lap. Cartier bracelet. Chanel bag. Gucci heels. By the end of two months, he dropped damn near 150k on me — cash, gifts, shopping sprees.

And I ain't let him hit once.

He bought me a diamond chain just so I'd "remember him" when I wasn't around. He wired money for a "vacation" I never took with him. One night, he handed me keys to a foreign like it was candy, grinning like, "You mine now."

I smiled sweet, kissed his cheek, and the next day I was in another nigga's section.

Tika used to sit on my bed, watching me unwrap boxes like it was Christmas. "Girl, you the devil," she laughed, shaking her head. "You got this man spending six figures and he ain't even sniffed the pussy yet."

I smirked, slipping a ring on my finger. "He don't even want the pussy, not really. He want the dream of me. And dreams? Dreams expensive."

And that was the truth. Every night he thought he was closer. Every week he went harder, dropping money like water.

But in reality? I was bleeding him slow, piece by piece, till there wouldn't be nothin' left but powder on his nose and a hole in his pockets. Because the game wasn't about who fucked who. The game was about who walked away richer.

And I wasn't leaving broke.

It wasn't the rapper with the coke habit that leveled me up — it was the ball player.

Name was Dre "MoneyBag Dre" Lawson, fresh off signing a big-ass contract. Six-nine, tatted, beard lined sharp, and pockets fat like he robbed a bank. He slid in my DMs like he was just another nigga, but by the second link-up, he was already showing me floor plans.

"Baby, you too fine to be stayin' with your auntie," he said, one hand on the wheel of his G-Wagon, the other on my thigh. "Pick a spot in Buckhead. I'ma put you where you belong. Phantum need a throne."

Two weeks later, I had keys to a high-rise condo — marble counters, glass balcony, skyline view like a movie, rent, bills, even my internet — all in his name.

I stood in the middle of that empty living room the first night, lights off, city glowing, and whispered to myself, "I made it."

Tika wasn't lettin' me breathe. "Bitch, you gotta celebrate! This a whole new level." She dragged in bottles and called everybody she knew.

By midnight, the condo was wall-to-wall with promoters, strippers, hustlers, even a couple other IG models who swore they was competition. Smoke clouded the air, bass rattled the windows. My page was blowing up in real time, tagged in everybody's story.

Then shit went left.

Rico Flame, the rapper with the coke nose and YouTube hit, showed up uninvited. He stumbled through the door, nose dusted, eyes glassy, chain crooked like it was choking him.

"Jas!" he shouted over the music. "You really havin' a party without me? After all the shit I done for you?"

The crowd froze.

Dre stood up slow from the couch, towering over everybody, jaw tight. "Nigga, who the fuck is you?"

Rico laughed, sniffing hard. "Who am I? Nigga, I'm the one she fuck with! You just the dummy payin' her rent!"

Gasps rippled through the room.

I stepped forward quick, hands out. "Yo, chill! Y'all wildin', it ain't even..."

But Dre wasn't listening. He shoved past me, eyes locked on Rico. "Say that shit again."

Rico's grin spread, wild. "You deaf, nigga? She mine. You just payin' to babysit."

Dre swung first, cracked him across the jaw so hard his chain flew sideways. The whole condo erupted. Bottles fell, women screamed, phones shot up in the air recording. Rico hit the ground, but one of his boys yanked a pistol out his waistband.

"Back the fuck up!" he yelled, waving it crazy.

Dre's boys rushed in too, steel flashing. Shots rang out — BOOM! BOOM! BOOM! The windows shook, glass shattered, somebody hit the ground screaming.

I hit the floor behind the kitchen island, heart slamming out my chest. Tika crawled under the counter next to me, eyes wide.

When it was over, one of Rico's boys was laid out bleeding from the leg. Dre's crew dragged him toward the elevator, cursing, promising payback.

Rico stumbled after them, jaw swollen, spitting blood. "Bitch, you gon' regret this! You playin' with fire, Jas! Watch!"

The condo reeked of smoke, liquor, and gunpowder. Sirens wailed somewhere outside. Broken glass crunched under my heels when I stood up, my dress torn at the side.

Tika grabbed my arm, shaking her head. "Girl...what the fuck did you just start?"

I fixed my hair in the reflection of the black TV screen, mask back in place. "I ain't start nothin'," I said cold. "They started it. I just collectin' the crown."

And deep down, I meant it.

Queens don't pick sides in wars. Queens just collect what's left when the bodies drop.

The morning after, my phone was on fire. Clips from the condo hit Instagram before the sun came up. Shaky-ass videos of Dre swingin' on Rico, bottles flying, guns flashing. WorldStar posted it with the caption: "Rapper Rico Flame Gets Folded By NBA Star MoneyBag Dre Over IG Model."

And in every angle, you could see me — dead center. Dress painted on, legs looking good as fuck, diamonds hittin' the light, calm as fuck, while chaos exploded around me.

Tika barged in, half-dressed, phone in hand. "Bitch! You all over the fuckin' internet. You famous-famous now!"

I scrolled through my notifications. Followers jumpin' by the thousands, comments stacked up like bricks. My name was everywhere.

Then came the bullshit. Rico's "main girl," some Miami chick who swore she was wifey, jumped straight in my comments:

"This hoe Phantum been fuckin' my man. Bitch a homewrecker. Industry mattress. Everybody know the truth now." Her little fan club followed, droppin' clown emojis, snake emojis, paragraphs about me being a hoe.

Tika fell on the bed laughing. "Not this dusty bitch tryna come for you! She mad her

cokehead nigga out here eatin' your pussy in
his Rolls while she sittin' at home broke."

I wasn't mad. I was annoyed. That's the
difference. Mad bitches lose control. Annoyed
bitches flip the script.

So I pulled up my gallery, picked the coldest
pic I had — me in the condo window, Buckhead
skyline behind me, wrist heavy with Cartier.
Caption: "Queens don't chase. They collect.
#Phantum"

I hit post.

Within an hour, the whole vibe shifted.
Crown emojis, fire emojis, girls writing
"GOALS" in all caps, niggas begging me to
check my DMs. The hate drowned in the flood.

That's when I knew. They could scream
"hoe," "snake," "thief" all day. Didn't matter.
Online, I was untouchable.

I wasn't just finessin' these niggas anymore.
I was runnin' an enterprise based on disguise.
And I wore the mask better than anybody alive.

CHAPTER
11

The Empire of Illusion

The night I met Donna, the club felt like a movie.

Neon lights bouncing off diamond chains, smoke heavy in the air, bottles popping like gunshots. Industry niggas everywhere — promoters, rappers, "producers" with laptops they never opened. Everybody trying to be seen.

Me? I was already being watched. IG fame had me glowing different. Dudes staring, girls whispering, cameras flashing when I walked past.

But Donna? Donna made noise.

"Bitch, move, you blockin' the bad ones!" she shouted, elbowing her way through the crowd, hips and ass swinging like she owned the floor. Skin caramel smooth, thighs thick, long nails clacking against her glass. Hair laid, body poured into a red dress that looked painted on.

She stopped dead in front of me, looked me up and down, and smirked. "You the Phantum bitch, huh?"

I raised an eyebrow, sipping my drink. "Depends who asking."

She laughed, loud and messy, head thrown back. "Oh yeah, that's you. Attitude on ice. I fuck with it."

Without asking, she slid into the booth next to me like we been cool for years. "Name's Donna. And lemme tell you right now — these niggas in here? All bark, no bite. But they pockets fat. You and me? We could have they ass buying out the whole mall by the weekend."

Tika leaned across the table, side-eyeing her. "And who the fuck is you?"

Donna didn't flinch. "The bitch that's gonna make y'all more money than y'all ever seen."

I watched her talk, hands flying, words slick, voice cutting through the music. Loud. Bold. No fear. She wasn't lying; the energy around her pulled eyes the way diamonds caught light.

By the end of the night, she had promoters sending bottles to the table, rappers leaning over to ask her name, and some old-head throwing a stack just to get her number.

She leaned into my ear, laughing. "Told you, sis. These niggas easy. They just need the right kind of bait. And you? You dangerous bait. Stick with me, and we'll bleed 'em all dry."

For the first time, I saw myself not just as a hustler, not just as Phantum. With Donna on my side, it felt like a whole empire could be built.

After that night, me and Donna moved like we'd been sisters forever. Wherever I went, she was right there — loud, thick, laughing too hard, shaking ass like it was currency. And truth was? It was.

The first lick we hit together was some industry promoter named Kenny. Fat chain, belly pokin' out his designer shirt, breath loud as his laugh. He thought he was the plug, bragging about how he "made" half the rappers in the city.

Donna slid up on him first, nails tracing his chest. "Damn, you smell like money," she purred.

His eyes lit up like Christmas. "You know I keep it on me, baby." He patted his pocket, flashing a thick roll.

I leaned in from the other side, whispering in his ear. "Bet you don't spend it like you talk it."

By the end of the night, he dropped five racks on bottles just for us to sit at his table...and he didn't even get a kiss.

Donna taught me quick — men ain't pay for pussy, they pay for the dream of it.

Sometimes we let 'em think they were close. Like Dre's homeboy, some slick-talking dude with veneers and a chain heavier than his career. He pulled us into his penthouse, and the coke lines already laid out on the glass table.

"Y'all bad as hell," he slurred, eyes bouncing between me and Donna. "I'd do anything just to taste."

Donna grinned, pushing him back on the couch. "Then taste."

We let him eat us out one after the other, his nose dusted white, his jaw working like he was starved. He begged to fuck, but the coke killed him — dick hard for five seconds, then limp like a wet noodle.

He was embarrassed. We weren't. 'Cause in the morning, there was a Louis bag and two stacks waiting for us on the dresser.

Week after week, the pattern repeated.

One nigga dropped jewelry. Another wired money just so I'd answer his call. Donna had this older sugar trick — white, balding, stinking of cologne — who paid her rent just to sniff her panties.

We laughed about it on the ride home, counting money in the back of cabs.

"These niggas stupid," Donna cackled, licking hot wing sauce off her fingers. "And we the smartest bitches alive. They think they in control 'cause they got money. But really? They funding our whole empire."

I nodded, scrolling my phone, new DMs stacked with blue checks. "Money don't move without pussy. And we got both."

And with every trick, every gift, every night of playing men against themselves, I felt it more: The mask wasn't just protection anymore. It was product. It was power.

And sex? Sex was just the bait on the hook.

It was Donna's idea first.

We was laid up in my condo, wings on the table, money spread out like a deck of cards. She was scrolling her phone, laughing. "Bitch, you see this? That punkass promoter Kenny just posted a stack on his story. Dumbass tagged the spot and everything. Like he ain't screaming, 'Come rob me!'"

I smirked, licking sauce off my finger. "He soft. Spendin' money just to be seen. Nigga ain't built for the streets."

Donna leaned forward, eyes flashing. "So why not make his dumb ass pay for real? Set him up. He already think you fuck with him. Lemme line it up."

I raised an eyebrow, like I ain't never done nothing like that. "You serious?"

She grinned, pulling a blunt from her purse. "Dead serious. Look, he's easy. Get him comfortable, bring him somewhere quiet, and my peoples gon' do the rest. We walk away rich, nobody knows shit. Phantum never in the picture."

I sat back, thinking. My stomach twisted, but not from nerves — from the rush. The idea of it had my pussy wet, like the first time I realized niggas would drop racks just to touch me.

"Alright," I said finally. "Let's do it."

It went down two nights later. I hit Kenny's line, soft voice dripping like honey. "Come through, I miss you."

He pulled up in a Range Rover, fat roll in his pocket, smelling like cheap cologne and ego. We kicked it in the condo for a while, him running his mouth about how many rappers owed him favors.

I played my part, sitting on his lap, kissing his neck, whispering in his ear like I couldn't wait to fuck. "You really like me, huh?" he grinned, hand on my thigh.

"Of course, baby," I purred. "Matter fact...let's ride. I know a spot." I texted Donna while he grabbed the keys. One word: Go.

We drove out past the city lights, Kenny laughing, talking about investing in me. "Phantum LLC, baby!" he hollered, high off his own bullshit. "We gon' make millions together!"

I smiled sweet, sliding my hand over his. "We already rich, papi." That's when the black SUV cut us off.

Doors flew open. Masks. Guns. Donna's cousins.

"Out the car, bitch-ass nigga!"

Kenny froze, stammering. "W-wait, wait, wait!" A pistol whipped across his jaw shut him up. Blood sprayed the dashboard.

I kept my face calm, slipping out the passenger side like I was just as shocked as him. Heart pounding, pussy throbbing from the adrenaline.

They snatched his roll, his watch, even his shoes. One of them pressed the barrel to his head, ready to end it.

"Yo, chill!" Donna snapped from the SUV. "Not here. Not tonight. Take the money, leave him breathing."

They tossed him on the ground, bloody and broken, then peeled off with the bag.

Back at the condo, money poured out the duffel bag like water. Stacks on stacks, bloodstained bills scattered on the floor.

Donna lit a blunt, laughing till tears rolled. "That dumbass thought he was about to wife you up. Nigga almost lost his life for some pussy he was never gon' get."

I counted the bills, hands shaking, heat running through my body like fire. My panties were wet — not from Kenny, not from sex, but from the power.

"Money and death," I whispered, staring at the stacks. "That shit turn me on."

Donna exhaled smoke, grinning wicked. "Then bitch, you addicted now. Welcome to the real game."

Word spread fast. Not about Kenny getting stripped, that stayed quiet 'cause Kenny wasn't about to admit he got robbed by a bitch. But about me and Donna? About how we moved? Everybody wanted us in the room.

Shit grew like a avalanche; a promoter hit my DM. "Yo Phantum, pull up this weekend. I'll drop 10k just to have you in the section. Post a story, tag the club, drinks on me."

I read it out loud. Donna nearly spit her drink. "Ten fuckin' racks to just sit there and look pretty? Bitch, we celebrities now!"

I shrugged, smirking. "Ain't nothing but a walk-through."

She clapped her hands, laughing. "No, ho, that's called a BAG. You better wear your thottiest fit, 'cause we draining these niggas dry."

We pulled up like stars. Matching fits, heels clicking, diamonds flashing. Cameras flashed soon as we hit the door.

Inside, bottles rained. Niggas fought just to send us liquor, just to get tagged in a post. Donna soaked it up, dancing on couches, hollering loud.

"Bitch, take this video!" she shouted, twerking on the table while stacks flew around her. "Caption that shit 'Queens Don't Beg!'"

I stayed cooler, mask on. I smiled just enough, posed just right, whispered sweet in ears when I needed to. But my mind was always counting. Who spending? Who sloppy? Who worth lining up later?

Between the two of us, it was perfect. She was the storm. I was the silence after.

The next morning free designer boxes showed up at the condo. Some boutique tagged me in a post, calling me their "muse." Donna snatched one of the bags, grinning.

"Girl, you realize we don't even gotta buy shit no more? Niggas and brands just handing it to us. We the product!"

I looked at my page, likes running up, comments full of crown emojis. She was right. This wasn't just hustling anymore. It was image, it was marketing, it was a whole empire built off smoke and mirrors.

"You loud as fuck," I told her, "but you right. The illusion pay more than the pussy ever could."

She laughed, slapping my thigh. "Bitch, we getting rich off captions. Fuck the rest."

And just like that, the brand grew bigger than the street. But the streets? They weren't done with us.

The penthouse air was thick — perfume, liquor, powder, and sweat. Money was everywhere, like confetti after a parade. The whole room smelled like excess.

A football player name Randy come over after the club. A trick that loved to spend on me big time. He laid flat under me, shirt open, chains clinking against his chest. His pupils were blown wide, lips dry, begging with his eyes like he couldn't live without me.

"Please, Jas... ride me. Don't stop." I didn't.

My ass bounced slow at first, deliberate, like I was teasing him with every inch. My thighs gripped tight, skin slick, body moving like music only I could hear. The sound of it filled the room — wet, rhythmic, obscene.

My titties bounced with each grind, diamonds catching the light every time they swung. My mouth hung open, moans spilling out raw and heavy. Not soft porn-star moans...real, gutter, almost ugly sounds that filled the air and made him claw at the sheets.

"Oh fuck... ohhh fuck...this pussy so good" he stammered, his voice breaking, his whole body twitching under me.

I leaned down, my lips brushing his ear, nails dragging down his chest hard enough to leave marks.

"You don't own me, baby. You never will. You just renting time."

The way he moaned at that? Like the words cut him deeper than my nails.

But it wasn't him I was focused on.

It was me.

The mirrors wrapped the room like a stage. Every bounce of my ass, every jiggle of my breasts, every shake of my hair was captured from all sides.

I watched myself ride him — head thrown back, moans echoing, pussy sounding like wet Mac and Cheese, body glowing like it was carved from gold.

And behind the reflection, I saw flashes in my mind: Kenny getting his jaw cracked, blood spraying across the dash. Donna's loud laugh as we counted dirty money on the condo floor. Guns waving, shots popping, chaos feeding the fire inside me.

The memories and the moment blended together. Sex, money, death.

And the higher I bounced, the louder I screamed, the wetter I felt.

It wasn't his dick making me cum. Hell, half the time it barely stayed hard from all the coke in his system.

It was the power.

It was the fact that this man would empty his bank account just to hear me moan. That he thought he was fucking me, when in reality I was fucking his whole ego, his whole business, piece by piece.

"Goddamn, Jas!" he cried, hands shaking, eyes glassy. "You perfect, you...fuck...I love you!"

I laughed, breathless, grinding harder till he shook under me. "You don't love me. You love the dream."

And when I came, it wasn't for him. It was for me. My moans echoed off the glass, high-pitched, uncontrollable, filling the whole penthouse like a siren. My body shook, titties bouncing, thighs locking around him tight.

The orgasm rolled through me like gunfire — quick, violent, unstoppable. I collapsed forward, lips brushing his neck, whispering between gasps: "Money make me moan. Power make me cum. Death keep me wet."

His whole body shivered at the words. He thought it was dirty talk. I knew it was prophecy.

When he finally passed out, sweating, weak, and mumbling my name like a prayer, I slid off him slow. My robe slipped back over my shoulders, silk kissing my skin.

I padded barefoot to the mirror, city skyline glowing behind me. My hair was wild, skin dewy, breasts still heaving. Diamonds glittered like stars across my body.

I raised my phone, snapped a picture — robe half open, money scattered across the floor, his limp body blurred in the background. Caption: "Queens don't fuck for love. They fuck the world for power. #Phantum"

By the time he even rolled over, my notifications were blowing up. Likes, comments, DMs, a digital crown landing on my head in real time.

And staring at my reflection, I knew the truth. I wasn't just a hustler anymore; I was a goddess of illusion. And every moan, every bounce, every dollar was worship at my altar.

CHAPTER
12

Love Costs Everything

The phone always rang the same way.
"You have a collect call from...CJ."
That voice used to make my stomach flip. Now?
It made me pause whatever game I was
running and put my mask on tight.

I pressed the phone to my ear, voice soft.
"Hey, baby."

CJ's voice came low, steady, same as always.
"What's good, Jas? You holdin' it down for
me?"

I glanced at the mirror across from my bed,
my hair still messy and thighs still trembling
from the night before. A rapper had just left,
the sheets still smelling like liquor, latex, and
sweat. Money was scattered across the dresser,
jewelry shining under the lamp.

I pulled the blanket higher, hiding it all from him like he could see through the line. "Of course, baby. Always."

He chuckled, a deep sound that still sent chills through me. "I know you, Jas. You slick. You dangerous. But don't let the streets eat you alive while I'm gone. You hear me? You mine. You always gon' be mine."

I closed my eyes, biting my lip. "I know." But in my chest, I felt that twist — guilt and lust wrestling. He was talking like I was his queen. Meanwhile, my pussy was still wet from another man's tongue.

CJ kept talking, dropping gems like he always did. "Rule number one," with voice firm, "Never let a nigga think he own you. Rule number two, never move sloppy. You don't owe nobody shit but yourself."

I whispered back, soft, "I hear you." But in my head, all I could hear was Donna laugh from last night, telling me I rode that nigga like a Bentley I didn't have to pay for.

When the call clicked off, I sat in silence for a long time. The room still smelled like sex and sweat. My phone buzzed on the nightstand — a new DM from another blue check, asking where I was.

I stared at CJ's name on the screen, then at the message lighting up under it. Love was one thing. But love didn't buy condos, diamonds, or keep the hunger out my chest.

The suite smelled like everything expensive — champagne spilling, cigars burning, leather couches soaking in smoke. Money was scattered across the king bed like confetti, stacks untouched in duffels on the floor.

And me? I was on top, riding a celebrity nigga like I owned the world.

His face was red, veins bulging, hands clawing at my thighs like he was drowning. My ass clapped against his waist, skin sticky with sweat, tits bouncing heavy in his face.

"Goddamn, Jas..." he gasped, voice breaking. "You different...you worth every fuckin' penny."

I moaned loud, raw, back arched, head thrown back. But it wasn't his words that made me louder. It was the diamond bracelet glinting on my wrist, the Cartier bag tossed on the dresser, the black card he gave me tucked in my purse.

Every thrust, every grind, every scream that ripped out my throat was tied to the money he spent.

"Faster, baby, please!" he begged, choking on his own breath.

I slowed down, smirking, moaning soft into his ear. "You want faster? Then buy me that Chanel I showed you. Tonight."

He groaned, desperate, nodding like a fool. "Done...it's yours, baby...it's yours!"

That's when I started bouncing harder, titties swinging, moans echoing off the suite walls like a soundtrack to his downfall.

When I came, it wasn't because of him. It never was. It was because of the money. Because of the power. Because I knew his whole career, his whole bank account, his whole image — all of it was bending under me.

The louder I screamed, the wetter I got. My nails dug into his chest, leaving marks he'd remember long after I was gone. And when he finally collapsed, shaking, begging me to stay, I slid off him slow, pulling his shirt over me like it was mine.

My phone buzzed on the nightstand, Donna, voice loud even through text: "BITCH! You better drain that nigga dry. I got us another play tomorrow."

I laughed, sipping champagne straight from the bottle, the taste mixing with the salt of sweat on my lips.

Luxury, lust, and the streets — it was all the same high. And I was addicted.

She lined up another prize. Some old-head "investor" type, white dude, balding, teeth too white to be real. He claimed he ran hedge funds, but really he just liked to spend his money on young pussy.

"He easy," Donna told me, licking sauce off her nails in the condo kitchen. "All he want is to be around bad bitches. Flash a little titty, laugh at his jokes, he'll hand you the keys to the vault. We gon' set him up nice."

I smirked, sipping my wine. "You sure he ain't protected? White boys with that kinda money usually got security."

Donna waved me off. "Girl, please. He dumb. He think his money protect him. That's the best kind."

We met him at a downtown lounge, me in a silk dress, Donna in something that barely covered her ass. He was already sweating when we sat down, eyes wide, trying to look young in his Gucci loafers.

"Ladies," he grinned, patting his belly. "You two are somethin' else. Damn near walked in here and stopped my heart."

Donna laughed loud, rubbing his arm. "Careful, baby. We don't need no heart attacks before dessert."

He chuckled, nervously wiping his forehead. "Drinks on me. Order whatever you want."

By the end of the night, he was slurring, bragging about his investments, flashing his Rolex like it was supposed to impress me. I leaned in close, nails brushing his chest.

"You talk a lot about numbers, papi," I whispered. "But I don't believe you unless I see it. You should show me sometime, somewhere private."

His pupils dilated, throat bobbing. "My condo's right around the corner."

Perfect.

The spot was slick, high-rise, white walls, everything smelling like money and cologne. He stumbled in with us, laughing, hands already shaking as he tried to pull Donna's dress up.

She pushed him back playfully. "Relax, papi. Don't rush it. Let's make it fun."

That's when the door burst open. Masks. Guns. Donna's people. "On the fuckin' ground!" one shouted, pistol aimed at his head.

The investor froze, hands up, mouth open. "Wh-what the fuck is this?! Jas?!"

I gasped, playing shocked, stepping back like I had nothing to do with it. My heart hammered, but my face stayed cold.

They snatched his watch, his wallet, tore through his drawers for cash. The old man started crying, voice cracking.

"Please! Please don't hurt me, take it all, just don't kill me!"

One of the masked men shoved him down hard, gun pressing into his skull. "Shut the fuck up!" The trigger pulled halfway — CLICK.

I flinched, my stomach flipping, but the adrenaline shot straight between my legs. My thighs clenched, breath heavy.

They didn't kill him. Not that night. But when we left, blood was dripping from his nose, his eye swollen shut, his condo torn apart.

Back in the SUV, duffel bag full of cash and watches on the seat, Donna lit a blunt, laughing.

"Bitch, did you see his face? White boy almost pissed himself!"

I was shaking, my nails digging into my thighs. Not from fear. From the high.

I whispered low, almost to myself: "That rush...it feel the same as when I cum."

Donna looked over, grinning wide. "That's 'cause it's the same thing, ho. Money, sex, blood — it all hit the same nerve. And now you hooked."

She wasn't lying. I was hooked.

The phone clicked, static spilling through. "You have a collect call from...CJ."

I answered quick, heartbeat heavy. "Yeah, I'll accept."

"Yo," his voice rolled through the line, low and steady like always. "What's up, Jas? You sound tired."

I curled up on the couch, staring at the city lights through the window. The condo smelled like weed and leather, Donna's laughter still echoing in my head from earlier. "I'm good. Just been running around."

"You eating? You taking care of yourself?" His tone sharpened. "Don't lie to me, Jas."

I smirked, even though tears pressed behind my eyes. "I'm eating. I got money, I got everything I need."

"Everything but me," he said, voice softening. "I think about you every night, girl. Every fuckin' night. You don't even know."

That cut me. For years I told myself I hated him for leaving me. For being careless, for getting caught, for letting the system swallow him whole while I was out here fighting for scraps. But hearing the ache in his voice? It melted something in me.

"I used to be mad at you," I admitted, surprising myself.

He went quiet. "Mad? For what?"

"For leaving me," I said. My voice cracked. "For making me do this shit alone. For not being there when Mama died...when Keekee..." My throat closed.

Silence. Then he spoke, steady, almost whispering. "Jas... I ain't leave you. I got caught. The streets did this to me. To us. If I had a choice, I'd be there every fuckin' night holdin' you down. You know that."

Tears spilled before I could stop them. My hand trembled against the phone. I whispered through the crying, "I know. I know, CJ. And I'm not mad anymore. I can't be. I still love you too much."

His breath hitched through the line. "Say that again."

"I love you."

A pause, then his voice came back, cracked and raw: "I love you too, Jas. You the only thing keepin' me sane in here. Don't you ever forget that. I don't care what you do out there, long as you don't forget who the fuck you belong to."

I laughed through the tears, shaking my head. "Nigga, you still bossy as hell."

"You love it," he shot back, a smile in his tone. And he wasn't wrong.

After the call, I pulled up the app without hesitation. Fingers steady, I dropped $5,000 onto his books.

"Eat good, baby," I whispered at the screen. "Live good. That's on me."

Watching the confirmation pop up, I felt lighter. The anger I'd carried for years gone. Replaced with love, deep and raw, the kind that only grows stronger in distance.

CJ wasn't gone. He was still mine.
And I was still his.

Even if the world thought Phantum was untouchable, deep down I was still Jas. And Jas still belonged to CJ.

Ink still drying on my new condo lease and inside it was still humming with leftover energy from the night before — money stacked on the counter, champagne bottles half empty, silk sheets tangled on my bed. I was naked under the covers, scrolling through my phone, DMs stacked with rappers, athletes, even a couple verified CEOs trying to fly me out.

But my mind wasn't on them. It was on CJ. I called into the dark, half laughing, half crying, "I love you, CJ...I really do. But this money, this life? It got me too."

The contradiction made me moan soft, almost like it turned me on. Power, sex, love, all wrapped together until I couldn't tell the difference anymore.

That's when I heard the knock.

Tika strolled in first, wearing sweats, her hair tied up, always looking regular but sharp with her eyes. Right behind her came Donna loud as usual, dripping in Fashion Nova, hoop earrings swinging, phone already recording as she walked.

"Yasss, bitch!" Donna hollered, twirling in the living room. "This the fuckin' condo? Ho, we made it!"

Tika laughed polite, side-eyeing me. "She loud as hell."

I smirked, grabbing a robe. "That's just Donna. She extra."

Donna plopped on the couch, legs wide, popping open a bottle. "Extra get you paid, sis! Y'all better learn!"

They talked, joked, even smoked together for a while. Donna told wild stories, had Tika laughing despite herself. But when Donna left — leaving a cloud of perfume and smoke behind her — Tika shut the door and turned to me.

"Jas...she fun, but I don't like her like that."

I raised an eyebrow. "Why?"

"She too extra. Too loud. Too messy. I don't trust bitches like that. They attract the wrong kinda heat."

I waved her off, pouring another drink. "Relax. She got connects. She about her bread. That's all I need."

Tika frowned, arms crossed. "All money ain't good money, Jas."

I rolled my eyes. "Here you go again."

"Na, for real," she pressed. "You think you in control, but people like her? They bring drama. Don't say I didn't warn you."

I didn't answer. I just sipped my drink, watching the city lights flicker across the condo glass. Because deep down, I knew Tika might be right. But I also knew Donna made me money. And in my world, money always came first.

CHAPTER 13

Breaking the Crown

The sun cut through the blinds, too damn bright for the night we'd just had. Empty bottles lined the counter, money still spread across the glass table, heels tossed like bodies after a war.

Donna was sprawled across the couch, still in last night's dress, one heel on, one heel off, snoring loud as hell. Tika sat in the armchair, hoodie pulled over her head, scrolling her phone with that tight look on her face.

I walked out the bedroom in a silk robe, hair messy, voice scratchy. "Y'all look dead."

Tika glanced up at me, then at Donna. "She damn near is. That bitch don't know how to sit down."

Before I could answer, Donna snorted awake, stretching loud. "Bitch, please! I am the party. Don't nobody remember the night unless Donna was there." She sat up, grabbed a handful of cash off the table, and fanned herself. "Look at this. Niggas throwin' rent money just 'cause I shook my ass. We living good, baby!"

Tika sucked her teeth, rolling her eyes. "You call that living? That's attention. Attention get you killed."

Donna laughed so hard she spilled cash on the floor. "Girl, you jealous. You ain't got no ass to shake, so you hating on mine."

"Jealous?" Tika leaned forward, voice sharp. "Nah, bitch. I just ain't dumb. I seen plenty loud hoes like you end up in handcuffs or coffins. You extra as fuck, and that shit gon' spill back on Jas."

The room went quiet.

I sat on the edge of the table, robe slipping off my shoulder, trying to cut the tension. "Chill, both of y'all. Ain't no beef. We all on the same team."

Tika looked at me hard. "No, Jas. We not. She on her own shit. I'm telling you now—keep her close, but don't trust her too deep. She gon' bring heat."

Donna rolled her eyes, stuffing money into her bra. "Whatever. While you preaching, I'm getting the bag. Jas know what's up." She winked at me, grabbing her purse. "Call me when you ready to get this real money, sis."

She blew a kiss and strutted out, perfume cloud trailing behind her.

The second the door clicked shut, Tika muttered under her breath, "I don't like that bitch."

I sighed, rubbing my temples. "You don't gotta like her. You just gotta respect the hustle."

Tika shook her head. "Nah, Jas. That ain't hustle. That's a bomb waiting to blow."

I didn't answer. But deep inside, I knew she wasn't just hating.

The phone buzzed that night. "You have a collect call from...CJ."

I slid into my room, shutting the door before picking up. "Hey, baby."

His voice came through, deep and steady. "What's up, Jas? You sound distracted."

I hesitated. He was sharp like that, always could read me even through a phone line. "I'm good. Just tired. Been running plays all week."

"Plays?" His tone shifted. "Who you running with?"

My stomach tightened. Images of Tika frowning and Donna laughing flashed in my head. "Nobody serious. Just some girls, keeping me company."

He went quiet, then breathed deep. "Jas, listen to me. You can fuck with niggas, you can finesse, you can build your little empire — but your circle? That shit'll make or break you. Don't let nobody close you wouldn't bleed for."

I bit my lip. "You saying I'm slipping?"

"I'm saying I know you," he said firmly. "You got a soft heart under that hard mask. You let the wrong bitch get too close, she gon' eat off you. Or worse...she gon' sink you."

My chest got tight. His words felt aimed straight at Donna, even though he didn't even know her name. "Don't worry," I said quickly, forcing a smile he couldn't see. "I ain't no fool. I got it under control."

"You better," he replied, voice dropping lower. "I can't protect you from in here. And I can't lose you to no sloppy shit. You hear me?"

"Yes, CJ."

"I love you, Jas," he said, softer now. "Always. But love don't keep you alive. Smart does."

When the line clicked dead, I sat there in silence, staring at the floor. His words echoed in my head: Don't let nobody close you wouldn't bleed for.

I thought of Tika — loyal, steady, always by my side. Then I thought of Donna — wild, flashy, dangerous as hell. And for the first time, I felt the crown slipping on my head.

Two nights later, Donna had me in the back of a sprinter van headed downtown. Music blasting, bottles popping, her laugh cutting through the noise like always.

"Bitch, you ready?" she yelled over the bass, shaking her ass in the aisle. "We about to run this club like it's our damn kingdom."

I smirked, adjusting the diamond choker around my neck. "Ain't we always?"

The van doors swung open, and cameras flashed before we even touched the sidewalk. Donna strutted out first, red wig swinging, nails flashing like daggers. I followed, mask cool, robe of confidence wrapped around me like armor.

Inside the club, promoters swarmed us. One stuffed a stack straight into my hand. Another whispered, "Just post a story, baby, tag the club, that's all I need."

Donna leaned close, grinning. "See? We don't even gotta shake ass no more. We the bag."

She pulled me into the VIP, snatched a bottle from a baller's section, and poured champagne straight down her throat while everyone cheered. Her energy was magnetic — reckless, loud, dangerous.

And I loved it. But across the section, Tika sat stiff, arms crossed, eyes cutting through the smoke. When I finally slid next to her, she didn't even look at me.

"You see how wild she moving?" she muttered. "Jas, this ain't finesse. This messy. She gon' get you caught up."

I sipped my drink, watching Donna grind on a promoter just long enough to snatch his wallet out his pocket. "She bringing money in. That's all that matters."

Tika shook her head. "All money ain't good money. You forgetting that. One wrong move and you outta here, either in cuffs or in a coffin. And she the type to make it happen."

I wanted to snap back, but the truth stung. Instead, I took another sip and turned away, letting the bass drown out her words.

The play was supposed to be smooth. Donna swore up and down. "This nigga a clown, Jas. He stay posting money photos on IG like he in a rap video. Soft as fuck. We go over there, sip a little, laugh a little, and then boom — bag secured. Easy lick."

I looked at her hard. "Easy licks don't exist. Stop saying that shit."

She rolled her eyes, sliding on her red wig. "Girl, please. You always so damn paranoid. That's why you need me. You the ice, I'm the fire. Let's go get this money."

The condo smelled like Hennessy and weed. Dude was already sloppy drunk, shirt half open, chain dangling. He grinned when we walked in, waving a thick roll like it was a trophy.

"Damn, two bad bitches at once? I must be blessed tonight!"

Donna giggled, sliding right into his lap, plucking bills from his hand like petals. "You blessed, baby. Real blessed."

I stood back, scanning the room. Something was off. Too many shadows, too many whispers in the corners. "Donna," I muttered, "this shit feel funny."

She shot me a look, fake smile still on her face. "Relax. We good."

That's when the door kicked open. BANG! The wood splintered, men in masks rushed in, guns up.

"On the fuckin' floor!" one screamed. The drunk dude panicked, reaching for something. A shot rang out — BOOM! Bottles shattered, glass flying. Chaos exploded.

I tried to duck behind the couch, but fire tore through my side. "AHHH! Fuck!" I screamed, clutching my ribs. Warm blood soaked my dress, running down my hip.

Donna voice cut through the noise: "Grab her! Grab her, we gotta move!"

Two of Donna's people pulled me up, my legs weak, blood dripping onto the carpet. Bullets still flying, screams bouncing off the walls.

"We can't stay here!" one of them shouted.

"Where we taking her?" the other asked, dragging me toward the door.

Donna snapped back quick: "To Doc. CJ's old spot. Now!"

I barely registered the sprint down the stairwell, the blast of cold night air, the SUV doors slamming. My head spun, vision blurry, every bump in the road making me groan in pain.

"Don't you fuckin' pass out, Jas!" Donna barked, gripping my hand tight. "Stay with me, bitch!"

I growled through my teeth, blood seeping fast. "Why the fuck they shooting at me, huh? This was your play, Donna! Who the fuck you really working for?!"

She hesitated, just for a second. Eyes flashing. Then she snarled, "Don't start that paranoid shit. Ain't nobody set you up. They wasn't supposed to shoot, alright? Just... just shut the fuck up and hold on."

I wanted to cuss her out, but the pain stole my words. My body shook as the SUV flew through backstreets, headlights bouncing off broken buildings and boarded-up homes.

We finally screeched to a stop outside a ragged two-story on the west side. Paint peeling, porch light flickering. Looked like death, smelled like cigarettes and old grease.

Donna pounded on the door. "Doc! Open up! It's an emergency!"

The door creaked open. A tall, tired man with gray in his beard squinted at us, eyes going straight to the blood soaking my dress.

"Damn, y'all bringing me corpses now?" he muttered. "Get her in, hurry."

They dragged me inside, laid me on a cracked leather couch. The whole place reeked of bleach and smoke. Medical supplies sat stacked in old crates, a pistol on the counter right next to gauze and needles.

Doc ripped my dress open at the side, shaking his head. "Bullet went clean through. She lucky. Could'a clipped her spine. Hold her down."

I screamed as he pressed gauze to the wound, sweat dripping down my forehead. Donna stood by the wall, pacing, nails tapping against her thigh.

"You good, Jas," she said, voice almost too calm. "Doc got you. Just breathe."

I glared at her through the haze, voice hoarse. "Tell me the truth, Donna...did you line me up? Did you set me the fuck up?"

She froze, eyes narrowing, then forced a laugh. "Girl, shut the fuck up. If I wanted you dead, you'd be dead. Stop talking crazy."

But the way her eyes slid off mine told me everything I needed to know. Maybe I was paranoid. Or maybe I wasn't.

Doc tied off the last stitch with a grunt, wiping his hands on a rag already soaked red. "You good now," he said flat, voice rough like gravel. "But don't move stupid for a while. You tear this shit open, ain't nothing I can do but watch you bleed out."

I groaned, teeth grinding, sweat sticking my hair to my face. "Thanks, Doc." He nodded once, lit a cigarette, and disappeared into the back room like he'd seen too many nights just like this.

The couch creaked under me as I shifted, pulling the blanket tighter around my body. Every breath was fire, every heartbeat a drum in my wound.

Donna stood in the doorway, arms crossed, eyes bouncing everywhere but me. "See? Told you Doc had you. You gon' be straight."

I stared at her. Long. Silent.

"Stop lookin' at me like that," she snapped. "I ain't set you up. Shit just got messy." I didn't answer. Didn't trust my voice not to break.

When she finally left, the house got quiet again, only the hum of a busted fan filling the space. I forced myself up, dragging toward the cracked mirror hanging crooked on the wall.

The glass split my reflection in pieces — hair wild, lips dry, skin glowing with sweat. My robe slipped, showing the fresh bandage on my ribs. Diamonds still clung to my wrist, glinting under the weak light.

I looked like a queen.

But I felt like a target.

The crown was mine, sure. But it cut deep.

I touched the bandage, flinching at the pain, and whispered to the broken reflection: "Queens don't break...but damn, this crown heavy as hell." Tears stung my eyes, but I wiped them quick, forcing a smirk. Because no matter how heavy it got, I wasn't taking it off.

Not now.

Not ever.

CHAPTER
14

Sitting Still, Dreaming Bigger

The couch in my condo felt more like a coffin. My ribs screamed every time I moved, stitches pulling tight where Doc sewed me up. I laid still, wrapped in silk sheets, staring at the ceiling while the city hummed outside my window.

For the first time since I was twelve, I wasn't moving. And it felt like hell.

Tika checked in on me, bringing food I barely touched. Donna popped in loud, cracking jokes, promising me I'd be back outside in no time. But inside? I wasn't laughing.

Getting shot shifted something. Made me realize this shit wasn't a forever hustle. The streets of Atlanta weren't nothing but a bigger version of Memphis. Same cycle, same snakes, same bullets flying.

I thought about Mama Denise, gone too soon. Keekee, swallowed by the game. CJ, locked behind bars. And me? I was starting to see the walls close in too.

But my heart beat stubborn, whispering the same thing every night when I closed my eyes: *You too big for this shit, Jas. Bigger than Memphis, bigger than Atlanta. You supposed to touch the world.*

Still, I didn't let the internet see me weak. Every morning, I propped myself up, covered the bandage with a designer fit, painted on a face, and snapped a selfie for IG.

"Another day, another bag #Phantum"

The likes poured in, comments full of fire emojis and crown symbols. Nobody knew I was stitched up, barely holding myself together. That was the game. You never let the world see you bleed.

But sitting still gave me time to think. Too much time. I had condos, cars, racks stacked to the ceiling. Men dropping jewels and gifts at my feet like I was a goddess. But it still felt small. Local. Basic.

What was I really chasing? Another club booking? Another lick with Donna's reckless ass? Another fight with Tika about who I could trust?

Nah. I wanted more. I needed more.

For the first time, I dreamed past the city lights. Past the South. Past the country.

I wanted international waters. And I had no idea that dream was about to walk right into my world.

The invite came on a night I wasn't even supposed to be outside. Bandages still fresh, Doc's words echoing in my ear, "Don't move stupid. Rest. Heal."

But rest never made me money. Rest never made me famous. And rest sure as hell didn't make me feel alive. Tika begged me to stay in. "Jas, sit yo ass down. You damn near died."

Donna laughed it off, waving the flyer like it was a golden ticket. "Girl, it's a private mixer at the St. Regis. Ain't no bullets in five-star hotels. We gon' be sipping champagne with millionaires. You need this."

I told myself I'd just show up, smile for a couple photos, and dip. Just enough to keep the illusion alive. But deep down, my pulse was already racing.

The St. Regis lobby smelled like money — fresh orchids, polished marble, expensive cologne trailing off men in tailored suits. My heels clicked against the floor, echoing like gunshots. Underneath the long black gown Donna made me wear, gauze hugged my ribs tight, each breath a reminder of how close I'd been to losing it all.

The elevator opened to the penthouse level, and instantly the air changed. Dim lights, soft jazz spilling from a live band, women in gowns that probably cost more than everything Mama Denise ever owned, men with watches heavy enough to break wrists.

I kept my chin high, mask flawless, each step purposeful. I wasn't Jas from Memphis tonight. I wasn't even Phantum the setup queen. Tonight, I was a fantasy, a goddess draped in silk and secrets.

Donna leaned into my ear, whispering, "See? This the level we supposed to be at."

And then I saw him.

He stood near the balcony doors, talking low with a cluster of men in suits. He wasn't tall, but he carried himself like height didn't matter. His beard was trimmed, salt-and-pepper, his thobe white as snow under the chandelier lights. A gold watch hugged his wrist, subtle but heavy. His voice was smooth, accented, and every man around him leaned in like his words were law.

When his eyes swept across the room and landed on me, my stomach flipped. This was not the look of lust; it was pure power, from a man used to owning everything he touched.

He excused himself from his circle and walked straight toward me.

Donna almost squealed. "Ohhh shit, bitch, you got him looking."

I whispered back, "Calm the fuck down." But my palms were already slick against my clutch.

"Good evening," he said when he reached me, his voice low, deep, carrying that rhythm only money can polish. "You don't look like you belong here."

My chin lifted. "Excuse me?"

He smiled, sipping his drink. "Everyone else in this room...I know their stories. I know their families, their business, their weaknesses. You..." He paused, scanning me like a jewel under a light. "You're a mystery."

Donna jumped in quick, her loud laugh slicing through the moment. "Mystery pays, don't it? She's Phantum — everybody wanna know her, nobody really do."

He chuckled, eyes never leaving mine. "Phantum. Interesting. Fitting."

I tilted my head, smirking just enough.
"And you are?"

"Kareem." He extended his hand, his ring flashing with each movement. "Oil, shipping, investments. My family's been in business longer than this city's been alive."

When I shook his hand, it wasn't soft. It was firm, confident, but respectful. The kind of grip that told me he didn't chase. He chose.

We sat in a quiet corner, Donna bouncing off to chase free champagne.

"So tell me," Kareem said, leaning back, studying me. "Why does a woman with eyes as sharp as yours waste them in rooms like this?"

I raised an eyebrow. "And what kind of rooms do you think I should be in?"

"Boardrooms. Palaces. Places where men move billions and wars are decided over dinner. Not nightclubs, not cheap promoters throwing cash like children."

His words cut deep. I sipped my drink to hide the way my chest burned. He saw right through me.

"I'm doing fine where I'm at," I said coolly.

He leaned forward, smile soft but dangerous. "No, you're surviving. But you... you were not made to survive. You were made to conquer."

My breath caught. He was right. I was
something else entirely. A queen with a
kingdom not yet claimed.

By the time the night ended, Kareem's
presence had wrapped around me like silk. He
didn't flirt the way American men did. No
begging, no boasting. Just steady, calculated
words that made me feel like stepping into his
world was destiny.

As the crowd thinned, he stood, adjusting
his cufflinks. "Come to Dubai."

I blinked. "Excuse me?"

He smirked. "You're wounded. Tired. You're
hiding it well, but I can see it in your eyes. Sit
still too long here, and these streets will eat you
alive. But with me? You'll see a different game.
Bigger. Cleaner. And more dangerous."

I hesitated. "Why me?"

"Because men talk to me like a rival," he
said simply. "But they talk to women like you
as if they're confessing sins. You can open
doors I cannot. In return, I'll show you how to
build an empire that makes everything you've
touched so far look...childish."

He slid a black card across the table. "First
class ticket. Tomorrow night. Decide."

On the ride home, Donna clutched my arm
like a kid at Christmas. "Bitch, did you hear

him? Dubai! Palaces, Bugattis, oil money! You better take that flight!"

I stared out the window, clutching the card tight. My ribs ached under the bandage, a reminder of how close I'd come to death. However, my mind was already drifting across oceans, seeing skylines I'd only ever scrolled past on Instagram.

That night, I stood in front of my mirror. Bandages still tight on my ribs. But my body wrapped in silk, my diamonds glowing.

From Memphis to Atlanta, I'd played the game on the streets. But Kareem's words wouldn't leave my head. You were not made to survive. You were made to conquer.

And for the first time, I believed it. I whispered to my reflection, "Memphis to castles. Why the fuck not?"

The black card was still sitting on my dresser like it was staring back at me. Every time I walked past, my eyes landed on it. It wasn't plastic — it felt heavier, like it could unlock the whole damn world.

But worlds come with prices.

My ribs still ached, stitches pulling tight every time I bent down. Doc told me to sit still, but how the fuck you sit still when a door that big just cracked open?

Donna barged in around noon, loud as ever, damn near kicking the door off its hinges. She had a shopping bag in one hand, a blunt in the other.

"Bitch, you ready for Dubai?" she hollered, tossing the bag on my couch like she already packed me.

I shot her a look. "Why you acting like it's your flight?"

"Because if it was, I'd already be gone!" she snapped back, lighting the blunt and pacing. "Do you even know what this means? Palaces, Bentleys, yachts bigger than this whole fuckin' block. You been settin' up dope boys and rappers — cute. But this? This oil nigga money? Different bracket. You better take that shit."

She flopped onto the couch, pulling the card off the dresser and holding it like treasure. "I swear, Jas, you crazy if you don't go. You sittin' here with bandages on, moving slow, when you could be riding camels with gold saddles and swimming in diamond pools."

I laughed, shaking my head. "You sound dumb as hell."

"Dumb?!" Donna puffed smoke, waving the card. "What's dumb is staying here waiting for another bullet. You want another hood doctor sewing your ass up? Or you want a real one in Dubai with ten nurses and a gold scalpel?"

Her voice echoed, and I couldn't deny it. She wasn't lying.

That night Tika slid through, hoodie up, lips tight. She didn't even sit. Just stood at the counter with her arms crossed, eyes cutting sharp.

"I heard," she said.

My stomach sank. "Heard what?"

"Don't play dumb. The Dubai nigga. Kareem. Donna running her mouth about palaces and Bugattis."

I sighed, sinking into the couch. "Why you always act like the fun police?"

"Because I give a fuck," she shot back. Her voice cracked, low but sharp. "Jas, listen to me. These rich men overseas? They not like these goofy ass rappers throwing chains. They don't play by no rules. You cross them, you don't get stitched up. You get vanished."

She stepped closer, her eyes hard. "Do you understand? Ain't no hood doctor saving you if this shit go left. They'll bury you in sand where nobody ever finds you."

I looked away, heart pounding. She wasn't lying either. "So whatchu think I oughta do, Tika?" I snapped. "Stay here? Keep fucking with promoters and athletes until somebody finally takes me out? Another setup, another shootout, another funeral? I'm tired of playing small."

She didn't answer, but the silence was louder than any words.

Later that night, the condo was quiet. Donna gone, Tika gone. Just me, the hum of the city outside, and that black card staring me down.

I stood in front of my mirror, robe falling open just enough to show the fresh bandage across my ribs. Diamonds still clung to my wrist, shining against the dull pain.

From Memphis to Atlanta, I'd survived. Hustled. Conned. Finessed. But Kareem's words wouldn't leave my head: You were not made to survive. You were made to conquer.

I leaned close to my reflection, eyes burning. "Fuck surviving. I want it all." I picked up the phone and dialed the number. My hand was steady now.

A smooth female voice answered. "Ms. Jas? Mr. Kareem has been expecting your call."

My heart skipped. "Tell him... tell him I'm in."

There was a pause, followed by, "The jet leaves at midnight. A car will pick you up. You won't need to pack — everything will be provided." Click.

I dropped the phone on the dresser, chest tight. Staring at the ceiling, I whispered to myself, "Stitches to thrones...eyes forward." And for the first time in weeks, I smiled.

Midnight came fast.

A black Maybach pulled up outside my condo, windows dark, driver in a sharp suit who didn't say a word. Just held the door open while I slid inside. My heart thudded the whole ride, bandage pulling with every breath, but I kept my face calm, my mask on.

The city lights blurred behind me as we sped toward the airport. I felt like I was leaving more than Atlanta; I was leaving the girl from Memphis who barely had shoes on her feet, leaving the setup queen who only knew club promoters and rappers. I was stepping into something I couldn't even name yet.

Sleek like a bullet, the white jet was waiting on the tarmac under the moon. Steps rolled down, a red carpet stretched across the concrete, and at the top stood Kareem.

He didn't wave. Didn't grin. Just stood with his hands clasped behind his back, like a king waiting for his queen.

When I stepped out the car, wind whipping my hair, I straightened my shoulders and climbed the stairs slow.

"Welcome," he said simply, extending his hand. His palm was warm, firm, guiding me inside like I belonged there.

The inside glowed soft gold. Leather seats hugged my body, crystal glasses sparkled on polished tables, the air itself smelled expensive — sandalwood and champagne.

I slid into the seat across from him, trying not to stare too hard at everything. "First time?" he asked, reading me easy.

I smirked. "On a private? Yeah. Usually I'm stuffed in coach with screaming kids."

He chuckled, pouring me a glass of champagne himself, not handing it off to staff, not acting above it. That said more than his watch ever could.

"To new skies," he said, raising his glass.

I clinked his, the bubbles sharp on my tongue. My chest tightened. This wasn't a hustle anymore; this was a new religion.

He leaned back, watching me. "Do you know the difference between rich and wealthy?"

I tilted my head. "Rich is money. Wealthy is...more money?"

He smiled like a teacher with a dumb student. "No. Rich is temporary. Rich buys cars, chains, condos. Wealth buys silence. Wealth buys governments. Wealth makes the law look the other way when you bend it."

I swallowed hard, his words settling in me like fire.

He continued, eyes steady, "I can make a man sign away his company without touching a gun. I can make a politician kneel without raising my voice. You want to play in my world, Jasmine? You must learn the difference."

Hearing him say my real name — not Phantum — made my skin tingle. Like he saw past the mask, straight into me. "I'm listening," I whispered.

Hours later, while the jet cut across the Atlantic, I walked to the window, staring down at nothing but black sky and stars. My reflection stared back at me, diamonds glinting, silk hugging curves, eyes sharper than they'd ever been.

When I turned, he was already smiling like he knew what I was thinking. Like he'd been here before with others. However, this time, I was the chosen one.

The jet touched down smooth, not like the rough jolts I was used to in coach flights. By the time we rolled to a stop, the sun was just breaking over the desert, a fireball spilling light across endless sand and glass towers stretching into the sky.

The air hit me as soon as the door opened — warm, dry, carrying hints of spice and oil. Even the breeze felt rich. A black Rolls Royce was waiting on the tarmac, driver in a suit bowing low.

Kareem gestured for me to step ahead, like he was presenting me to his world. I slid into the backseat, leather soft, stars twinkling in the roof, my skin tingling against the cool air.

As we pulled onto the highway, my eyes widened. Skyscrapers taller than anything in Atlanta rose in clusters, glass glittering like diamonds. Billboards flashed Chanel, Cartier, Rolex. Ferraris and Lamborghinis zipped past like it was normal.

Kareem watched me watch it all. "Do you see, Jasmine?" he said softly. "This is what happens when men dream without limits."

I couldn't even answer. My chest was too full.

We pulled up to a tower so tall it looked like it scraped the heavens. Inside, gold lined the walls, chandeliers dripping crystal, marble floors shining so bright I almost saw my reflection.

The suite was bigger than my entire condo back in Atlanta. Floor-to-ceiling windows overlooked the city, a king-sized bed sat draped in silk, a balcony reached out toward the desert horizon.

A butler handed me a glass of fresh juice like I was royalty. I turned slow, drinking it all in, heart pounding. This wasn't survival. This wasn't hustling rappers for purses or setting up promoters for cash. This was empire energy.

Kareem's voice floated behind me, calm and assured: "From Memphis streets to Dubai skies. Remember this moment, Jasmine. Because today you stop being who you were."

That night, after he left me to rest, I stood on the balcony alone. The city glittered like stars flipped upside down, highways lit like veins of gold. The wind whipped my hair, carrying the scent of spice and salt.

I touched the railing, eyes burning. Mama Denise's voice flashed in my head. Keekee's face. CJ's hands. Every memory of pain, every gunshot, every fight to stay alive.

And now... this.

I whispered into the night, "I ain't ever going back. Not Memphis. Not Atlanta. Not the girl who had to beg or bleed. I'm a queen now. And queens don't break." The desert wind carried my words away, but not their meaning. I held it inside like a mantra.

CHAPTER
15

White-Collar Crime

The morning after I landed, I woke to the sound of call to prayer echoing faint across the city. The sun poured through the windows, painting the skyline in gold. For a second, I thought I was dreaming. Then I rolled over, felt the silk sheets, and remembered — nah, this was real.

A knock came at the door. Kareem's assistant, slim in a sharp suit, bowed slightly. "Mr. Kareem will see you now." I slid out the bed, wrapped myself in a robe, and followed him through a maze of marble halls.

Kareem was waiting on the balcony of a high-rise office sipping dark coffee like it was wine. Below us, the city pulsed; Bugattis and

Bentleys crawled through streets lined with gold-plated signs.

"Sit," he said, motioning to the chair across from him.

I took the seat, back straight, pretending I belonged there, even though my heart was racing.

"You've been playing in small ponds, Jasmine," he said smoothly, his accent rolling over every word. "Clubs, rappers, promoters. Cute games. But money?" He leaned in, tapping the table with his ring. "Real money doesn't live in nightclubs. It lives in silence."

I frowned. "Silence?"

He smirked. "Guns make noise. Chains make noise. Even rappers, shouting about their cars and women — that's noise. And noise always ends up with enemies. But silence?" He paused, letting the word hang heavy. "Silence builds empires."

My stomach flipped. He wasn't talking like a hustler. He was talking like God.

Kareem leaned back, his eyes fixed on mine. "My family doesn't rob banks. We own the banks. We don't sell drugs. We control the companies that make the medicines. We don't kill our enemies with bullets. We kill them with contracts."

I swallowed hard, my fingers gripping the edge of the chair.

He smiled, slow and knowing. "This is the game you've been searching for, isn't it? Bigger targets. Bigger dreams. You have beauty, charisma, and mystery. Men will show you their weaknesses because they think you cannot use them. That is your power. And I will teach you how to use it."

The air around us felt heavy, like the whole city was leaning in to listen. "So what's my part?" I asked, steady but curious.

"You," he said, pointing at me with his ringed finger, "will sit at tables where men worth billions dine. You will smile. You will drink. You will listen. And while they drown themselves in your beauty, I will drown them in contracts. You don't need to understand the details. You just need to make them talk. Make them careless. Make them forget I am listening."

His words made my skin prickle. I wasn't just a hustler anymore. I was bait. I was leverage. I was the mask.

"And when it works?" I asked.

His smile widened. "When it works, you'll touch money you've never dreamed of. Not hundreds. Not thousands. Millions. Tens of millions. More."

He poured me a glass of that black coffee, sliding it across the table. "This is your initiation," he said. "Drink, and you leave your old world behind. Refuse, and I send you home tonight."

I picked up the glass, stared into the dark liquid, then lifted it to my lips. Bitter, strong, burning all the way down.

When I set it back down, Kareem's eyes glinted. "Good. Welcome to the empire, Jasmine."

The next afternoon, Kareem's driver rolled up in something that didn't even look like a car. It looked like the future.

A Bugatti Chiron, royal blue with chrome trim so clean I could see my reflection in it before I even touched the door. The engine purred low, like a beast growling in its chest, hungry.

"Get in," Kareem said, holding the passenger door with a slight nod, like this was nothing.

I slid inside, and the seat swallowed me whole. Butter-soft leather gripped my thighs, the kind of soft you don't get from malls or boutiques but from animals bred only for billionaires. The smell hit me — new leather, clean, mixed with the faint musk of Kareem's cologne. Something dark, expensive, and powerful.

The dash lit up in glowing blue, Arabic letters flowing across the screen. The second he tapped the gas, the world disappeared.

The Bugatti shot forward like a bullet, pinning me back in the seat so hard I gasped. The desert highway stretched ahead like a ribbon, and towers flashed past in blurs of silver and glass.

"Zero to sixty in two-point-five seconds," Kareem said calmly, his hand steady on the wheel. "This is not transportation. This is domination."

I couldn't stop laughing, breathless, my fingers clawing at the leather. "Shit! I damn near left my soul back at that light!"

His eyes slid to me, amused. "Do you feel it? The power?"

"Hell yeah, I feel it."

He smirked, turning the wheel sharp. The Bugatti hugged the road like it was glued, the tires whining, engine screaming. "Wealth is like this car. Fast, unstoppable, untouchable. Used properly, it makes men bow. Used recklessly, it kills you. Remember that, Jasmine."

We pulled into an underground garage stacked with more wealth than a rap video — Lamborghinis lined up like Skittles, Rolls Royces parked like taxis, a Ferrari with doors stretching toward heaven. I thought I'd seen rich before. I hadn't.

The elevator ride up was silent, Kareem standing still, hands behind his back like a king surveying his castle. When the doors opened, I damn near forgot how to breathe.

The penthouse wasn't just a suite. It was a palace in the sky.

Marble floors polished so slick they looked wet. Walls draped with handwoven silk, shimmering under crystal chandeliers bigger than any room I'd ever lived in. A floor-to-ceiling window stretched across the entire wall, revealing the Persian Gulf glittering under the sunset like liquid diamonds.

On the bed, a row of velvet boxes waited. Jewelry. Kareem lifted one, opened it, and slid it toward me. A diamond necklace, thick and heavy, each stone catching the light like fire.

"Pick what you like," he said simply, pouring himself a drink of something aged and amber.

I hesitated, then lifted it, the weight dragging my neck forward. The cold of the stones bit into my skin, sending a shiver racing down my spine.

I caught my reflection in the mirror: not Jas from Memphis, not Phantum from Atlanta. A queen. A goddess.

For the first time, I didn't just wear luxury. I was luxury.

Dinner that night was on a rooftop above the city, the entire floor reserved for us. A table stretched long, draped in white silk, plates lined in gold. Waiters moved like shadows, silent, sliding trays across the table with precision.

Kareem didn't even look at the menu. He ordered in Arabic, his voice smooth, commanding. Moments later, platters appeared — lamb roasted until the meat fell off the bone, rice jeweled with saffron and pomegranate, silver bowls of fruit glowing under candlelight.

When I tasted the first bite, the flavors hit me so hard I closed my eyes. Sweet, savory, spiced in ways I didn't even have words for. Back home, dinner was wings in Styrofoam boxes. Here? Every bite tasted like power.

Kareem watched me, a smirk tugging at his lips. "Do you see? This is not food. This is proof. This is what men with power consume every day. They believe they are untouchable, immortal, chosen."

I swallowed, licking saffron from my lips, heat rising in my chest.

"They make mistakes," he continued, sipping his wine. "Because when a man feels chosen, he underestimates everyone else. Including a woman sitting across the table, smiling at him. That is your weapon."

His words landed heavier than the diamonds on my neck. I ain't a hustler no more. I'm an empire.

Kareem's world wasn't velvet ropes and promoters — it was prime ministers, oil magnates, and bankers with egos bigger than their accounts.

First mark? Pierre Dufort. French banker. Round belly, red cheeks, watch fat enough to choke a wrist. He was known for two things: big deals and bigger mouths when the wine flowed.

The dinner was at a private yacht, docked in the Persian Gulf, lights bouncing off the black water like jewels. The deck smelled of sea salt and cigars, lined with waiters in white gloves carrying trays of champagne and caviar.

"Stay close, but don't crowd me," Kareem whispered as we walked up the yacht's steps.

His thobe fluttered in the ocean breeze; my gown clung to my curves like it was painted on. Diamonds heavy on my neck.

"You are not decoration, Jasmine," he said firmly. "You are distraction. They will talk to you, thinking you are harmless. You smile. You listen. And you repeat it to me later. Understood?"

I nodded, mask tight. "Understood."

The second we stepped onto the deck, eyes landed on me. French, Arab, British — didn't matter. Men with billions in their pockets suddenly forgot their deals. All they saw was me.

And that was the point.

Monsieur Dufort waddled over, already tipsy, bow tie loose. His eyes skimmed Kareem once, then stuck on me like honey. "Mon dieu," he said with a sloppy grin. "Who is this vision?"

Kareem's face didn't flinch. "My associate."

"Associate?" Dufort chuckled, leaning too close, wine on his breath. "Such beauty should not be wasted on business."

I tilted my head, lips curling into a sly smile. "Maybe beauty is the business."

He laughed so loud heads turned. "Ahhh, I like her." We drifted toward a quiet corner. "Tell me, cherie, do you enjoy yachts?"

I sipped my champagne, eyes locked on his. "I enjoy whatever men with yachts enjoy. But I enjoy secrets even more."

That made him blink. Then smirk. Then lean in further, whispering like we were already lovers.

"My bank...has certain contracts. Hidden funds. Offshore. But do not tell your...associate." He chuckled, glancing at Kareem, who was calmly discussing politics with another guest, pretending not to hear. "We French, we know how to make oil look like gold on paper, eh?"

I laughed softly, brushing his hand off my thigh with a playful push. "Men always want to tell me their secrets. I never ask. They just...fall out."

He grinned, teeth wine-stained. "Then you are dangerous, cherie. I like dangerous women."

By the end of the night, Monsieur Dufort was drunk, red-faced, and babbling about "unseen reserves" and "quick approvals." Every word he dropped was gold, and I caught it all.

Back at the penthouse, I relayed every detail to Kareem. The Frenchman had practically outlined his bank's weak points, bragging about accounts set up for Middle East oil speculation.

Kareem listened in silence, pouring whiskey, nodding slowly. "Excellent."

The next morning, a flurry of contracts went out. Kareem's lawyers drafted "investment proposals" for a fake oil field in Oman. Dufort, greedy and blinded by my smile, signed without hesitation.

The numbers blurred my vision: $20 million into Kareem's offshore accounts. Clean. Silent. Untouchable.

My cut?

One million. Wired straight to an account with my name.

When Kareem handed me the paperwork, I stared at the screen until my eyes burned. Seven digits. More money than my entire hood ever saw in a lifetime.

A girl from Memphis. A setup queen turned bait in a billion-dollar scam. And now? A millionaire.

Kareem raised his glass. "Congratulations, Jasmine. You've made your first million. The first one is always the sweetest."

I laughed, but it came out shaky. "It don't even feel real."

He leaned close, his voice a whisper sharp enough to cut glass. "It feels real when you spend it. But remember — it is not the million that matters. It is what you become to get it."

The screen still glowed with those seven digits, but I wasn't staring at it like some wide-eyed rookie. I'd already adjusted. Money was money.

What I felt wasn't shock. It was hunger.

The champagne Kareem poured barely touched my lips before my mind was racing again. Who's next? What's next?

Kareem leaned back in his chair, calm as a monk, smoke curling from his cigar. "Most people savor their first million," he said. "They waste it on toys, women, distractions."

I tilted my head, eyes sharp. "I ain't most people. One lick just makes me hungrier for the next. So line it up."

He chuckled, low and approving. "Good. I chose correctly."

He slid a thin folder across the table. Inside: photos of another mark. An oil consultant from London, always surrounded by security but known to gamble and drink until his guard dropped.

"He will be here for a conference," Kareem explained. "Arrogant. Careless. Easy prey if

159

played correctly. And this time, Jasmine...you will not only be the distraction. You will lead the conversation."

My chest tightened, not from fear, but thrill. "So I'm not bait," I smirked. "I'm the blade."

His slow nod said it all, but he emphasized, "Exactly."

That night, I laid in my suite, diamonds still clinging to my skin, eyes wide open. A million already in the account, but I didn't feel full. I felt empty and greedy at the same time.

This wasn't about proving myself to Kareem anymore. This was about proving something to me. From Memphis porches to Dubai yachts, I wasn't just surviving. I was building a throne, one sucker at a time. And now that I'd had a taste? I wanted it all.

The London oil consultant was a different breed from the French banker. Lean, pale, hair slicked back like an old movie villain. Armani suit hugging a body that sweated too much under Dubai heat. His security team hovered like shadows, but he kept pushing them back, craving space, craving attention.

And that's where I slid in.

Kareem set the stage at a private high-roller casino, the kind where even the chips looked heavy enough to pay rent for a year. Gold tables, champagne flowing, women in gowns brushing past, whispering promises.

I strode in slowly, gown slit high, heels clicking like gunshots. Every head turned. But my eyes stayed on the consultant.

He noticed. Of course, he did.

By the third hand of baccarat, he was beside me, breathing whisky fumes, flashing cards like he owned the room. "You believe in luck, darling?" he asked, placing a stack of chips at least ten times my aunt's rent on the table.

I leaned close, letting my perfume hit him, my thigh grazing his leg. "I don't believe in luck. I believe in leverage."

His pupils widened. Hook. Line. Sinker.

Over the next week, I bled him slow. Dinners. Drinks. Walks along the marina where I let his hand brush my hip but pulled away just enough to keep him chasing. Nights in his penthouse where I let him strip me down to lingerie but never let him inside — just his mouth, his tongue, his desperation while he begged.

Every time he came up for air, I whispered about opportunities. A field, a deal, "a friend of mine" who could connect him to the right contracts.

By the time he signed Kareem's papers, he wasn't just horny, he was obsessed. Obsessed enough to wire $50 million into accounts he barely understood.

Kareem poured champagne when the transfer cleared, his calm mask breaking into a grin. "Fifty million. You have surpassed every expectation, Jasmine."

My cut? Twenty-five million. More money than Memphis, Atlanta, and every hustler I'd ever met combined.

But while he raised his glass, I already had my phone buzzing in the pocket of my gown.

Another man. Another billionaire. One Kareem didn't know I'd been texting, meeting, planting seeds with while he thought I was 'resting.' I smiled at Kareem, clinking my glass against his. "To empire," I said out loud.

But in my head? To mine, not yours.

CHAPTER
16

The Mask Slips

The night after the oil consultant deal cleared, Kareem had me draped in silk at a rooftop restaurant that overlooked all of Dubai.

He leaned back in his chair, calm, sipping on whiskey older than my mama would've been. "Do you see what I've given you, Jasmine?" His eyes lingered on me like I was some rare jewel he'd discovered. "You were chasing scraps in clubs. Now you're dining with kings. You are everything because I made you see what you were capable of."

I smiled, tilted my head just right, let the candlelight hit the diamonds on my neck. "You right, Kareem. You opened the door."

But in my head? I laughed. He thought this was his empire, thought I was his prize student.

Nah. I was already drawing up blueprints for my own.

Kareem talked about the next plays, how "we" would move money through new shell companies, how "we" would bait more bankers. Every time he said "we," I nodded, eyes locked, lips curved in just enough admiration to stroke his ego.

Truth was, I wasn't listening. Not really. I was studying him.

The way his bodyguards shifted every time he lifted his glass. The way his phone never left his right pocket. The way he had to clear his throat before every lie.

I filed it all away.

"Stick with me, Jasmine," he said, leaning forward, that same calm menace in his tone. "And you'll never have to touch the dirt of the ghetto again. You'll be untouchable."

I raised my glass to his. "To never touching dirt again."

Our glasses clinked, crystal ringing out against the skyline. He thought it meant loyalty.

To me, it sounded like goodbye.

His name was Anton Vale. Tech billionaire out of Moscow. Younger than Kareem by a decade, sharper jawline, leaner build, but with a nervous energy like he always needed something to keep his hands busy. He wasn't oil money. He wasn't old money. He was new money — and new money is always hungry.

We met at a private lounge tucked inside a five-star hotel, the kind of spot that didn't even have a name on the door. Just a black marble wall, a man in a suit at the entrance, and a hallway that opened into a room where the cheapest drink probably cost five hundred dollars.

Anton was already at a corner booth, tapping at his phone like the world might end if he put it down. When he looked up and saw me, he froze. "Jesus," he muttered, sliding out the booth. "You're...stunning."

I gave him a slow smile, practiced in mirrors and hotel elevators. "You must be Anton."

"Yes, yes—please, sit," he said quickly, motioning to the booth like he was pulling out a throne. His accent clipped, his suit too tight in the shoulders, Rolex glinting under the low lights.

I slid into the seat, crossing my legs slow, letting my dress ride just enough to catch his eyes. He looked, tried to look away, then looked back. Hook set.

Anton cleared his throat, trying to act smooth. "Kareem mentioned you...briefly. Said you were learning the game. But he didn't tell me you'd be..." He trailed off, hand flicking in the air like words failed him.

"Pretty?" I said, arching a brow.

He laughed nervously. "That doesn't even begin to cover it."

I leaned closer, perfume wrapping him like smoke. "Kareem likes to keep me in the shadows. Says men talk too much around me if I'm in the room."

Anton tilted his head, studying me. "And do they?"

I smirked. "Every time."

He chuckled, taking a sip of scotch. "Dangerous. I like dangerous."

I let the silence stretch, sipping my wine slow, giving him time to stew in his own thoughts. Men like Anton? They hate silence. They fill it with secrets.

Sure enough, he leaned in. "I have access Kareem could never dream of. Banking tech. Crypto before the world even knows how to regulate it. And I—" he stopped, catching himself, shaking his head. "Sorry. I shouldn't be telling you this."

I placed my hand on his, soft but firm. "Maybe you should."

His breath hitched. He searched my eyes like he was trying to figure out if I was real. "Why do I feel like I've known you longer than ten minutes?"

I smiled, leaning close enough for my lips to almost brush his ear. "Because I make men feel comfortable before I cut them open."

He shivered. I could feel it through the table.

By the time dessert hit the table, Anton was practically begging to impress me. "I could set up something," he said, voice low, eager. "An offshore wallet. Crypto transfers nobody can trace. You'd have access. Real access. Not just crumbs Kareem sprinkles."

I tilted my head, playing coy. "And why would you do that for me?"

"Because..." He swallowed, licking his lips. "Because I want you to trust me more than you trust him."

I let that hang in the air, smirking as I sipped my wine.

Inside, I was screaming with laughter. Another billionaire, another fool, handing me keys to the kingdom just because I made him feel like maybe one day he'd get between my legs.

When the night ended, Anton walked me to the car. His body leaned close, lips inches from mine.

"Next time, dinner at my villa," he whispered. "Private. No interruptions."

I kissed his cheek slow, leaving a stain of lipstick. "Next time."

The car door shut, and as the driver pulled away, I leaned back in the seat, grinning into the dark.

Kareem thought he was my teacher. Anton thought he was my savior. Neither of them knew I was already running the board.

Anton came on strong after that first dinner. Flowers, gifts, calls at all hours of the night. The kind of attention that would've smothered me if I wasn't already three steps ahead.

"You're too special to be stuck in Kareem's shadow," he told me one night over the phone, his voice low and desperate. "Let me show you what it feels like to own something that's only yours."

My pause lingered as I pretended to consider it, followed by a soft but sharp: "Prove it."

Anton's villa looked like something out of a billionaire catalog. The drive alone had me dizzy — white marble gates sliding open like I was royalty, palm trees lit with gold lights, fountains throwing water into the desert air like it wasn't precious.

Inside, it was glass and steel everywhere, walls hung with abstract art he couldn't even name but bragged about anyway. A Bugatti and two Ferraris sat in his garage like toys.

He greeted me barefoot, linen shirt loose, trying hard to look casual. But the Rolex peeking out his sleeve and the sweat on his palms gave him away. He was eager. Too eager.

"You look dangerous tonight," he said, handing me a glass of Dom Pérignon.

I smirked, letting my perfume do the rest. "That's because I am."

He laughed nervously, shifting from foot to foot. "God, you drive me crazy."

Dinner was nothing but bait. By dessert, Anton couldn't keep it in.

"I wasn't joking about the offshore accounts," he said, sliding a tablet across the table like it was a love letter. Numbers filled the screen. Zero after zero after zero.

"All untraceable. Crypto wallets. Anonymous. Untouchable." His voice dropped.

"I could put two million in one for you tonight. Yours. No Kareem. No middlemen. Just us."

I stared at the screen, heart pounding. Not because I was nervous...because I wanted more. I dragged my eyes up to his, slow and steady. "Two? That's cute." I sipped my wine. "Make it five."

He froze, blinked, then laughed like I'd just told the filthiest joke. "You don't play fair."

"I don't play at all," I said, leaning close enough for him to smell the sweetness on my lips.

He swallowed hard. "Done."

Minutes later, he tapped a few keys, and just like that, five million dollars sat in a digital wallet with my name on it. No Kareem. No cut. Just mine.

The drive back to the city felt unreal. My phone buzzed with confirmation, my chest tight with adrenaline. Not street money. Not club licks. Not promoter scams. Real money. Digital. Global. Untouchable.

I walked into Kareem's penthouse later that night dripping heavier — new diamonds on my wrist, my smile sharper. And that was the problem. I didn't even realize I was glowing too hard.

Kareem noticed.

We sat on his balcony the next morning, the gulf stretching out calm and endless. He sipped his coffee slow, eyes cutting into me like knives.
"You're glowing," he said finally.
I smirked, trying to play it cool. "Maybe I'm just happy."
His gaze didn't move. "Happiness doesn't deposit five million into accounts I don't control."
My stomach dropped, but I didn't blink. "What are you talking about?"
He leaned back, swirling his cup, that calm menace in his tone. "I built this empire on silence, Jasmine. Nothing moves in my world without me knowing. Nothing. And yet..." He tilted his head. "You're sitting here in diamonds I didn't buy, sipping coffee like a queen I didn't crown."
I laughed, soft and fake. "You paranoid, Kareem. If I wanted to play you, don't you think I'd be smarter about it?"
That made him chuckle, low and dangerous. "That's the thing about smart women. They

think cleverness can hide hunger. But hunger always shows."

The air between us froze. He didn't push further. He didn't need to.

My mask was still on, smile tight, body loose, but inside? My heart was racing. I'd slipped. Just once.

And in Kareem's world, once was enough to get you buried.

It was past midnight when I slipped out my suite, robe dragging across marble, glass of red wine in my hand. Kareem's estate stretched wide and endless — too many doors, too many shadows. I wasn't looking for nothing. Just wandering, restless, that itch in my chest I could never shake.

That's when I heard it.

At first, I thought it was the wind. Low, hollow. Then it grew. Choked, muffled screams pushing through the cracks of the walls. My stomach flipped.

I followed. Every step felt heavier, the wine glass trembling in my hand. Past one hall, then another, until the air itself felt colder. Two guards stood by a narrow corridor, eyes forward, stone-faced. They didn't stop me, didn't blink, like they already knew curiosity was death, like they were daring me to keep walking.

I should've turned back. Memphis instinct told me, bitch, don't do it. But another part of me — the same part that had me hustling promoters and rappers, the part that had me chasing millions — couldn't help it.

The screams dragged me forward. I came to a heavy steel door, cracked just enough for light to leak out. I pushed, just a little, and peeked.

And froze.

Kareem stood inside, thobe sleeves rolled to his elbows, calm as Sunday morning. His voice? Smooth. Soft. Almost gentle.

"You stole from me," he said in Arabic, words I didn't fully understand but tone sharp enough to cut bone. "And now you pay."

The man in the chair was barely breathing. Shirt ripped, face swollen, blood dripping down onto the floor in slow, steady taps. One toe was missing, the stump raw and oozing. His eyes rolled back, but Kareem grabbed his chin and forced him to look up, calm as ever.

Then Kareem nodded once. His man stepped forward, blade in hand, slow and surgical.

I slapped my hand over my mouth, teeth digging into my palm to keep from screaming. My heart was banging against my ribs so hard I thought the guards outside might hear it.

I stumbled back, the robe slipping off my shoulder, wine glass shaking so bad it almost shattered. My throat was dry, stomach twisting, vision tunneling.

I'd seen niggas shot before. I'd seen overdoses, fights, even bodies in alleys. But this? This wasn't the streets. This was hell.

And the devil himself was running it.

Back in my suite, I slammed the door, back pressed against it, gasping like I'd just run ten blocks. My hands shook so hard I spilled wine down the front of my robe, but I couldn't even care. My ears still rang with those screams, that calm voice, that blade slicing.

"Fuck," I whispered into the dark. "Fuck, fuck, fuck."

The mask slipped. For the first time since I touched Dubai soil, I wasn't the cool, smiling queen. I was Jasmine from Memphis, knees weak, breathing ragged, scared as hell.

Because now I knew. Kareem wasn't just a hustler. Wasn't just a slick talker with bank connections. That man was a goddamn executioner. And if he ever caught wind that I was playing him on the side?

I pictured myself in that chair. My toes gone. My screams muffled in the same marble basement.

"No," I hissed, pacing the room, robe dragging, diamonds clinking around my neck. "I ain't dying in no foreign basement for no nigga. Not me."

I sat on the bed, hands gripping the sheets, brain racing. I had options now. Thirty-five million in cash. Ten million in crypto. My Rolls Royce already on a ship bound for Atlanta. Closets of designer stacked in crates. I had the money. I had the escape route.

And I had the fear.

The kind of fear that makes you move fast, before somebody else makes the decision for you.

I looked out the floor-to-ceiling window, Dubai glittering like a jewel box below. It was beautiful. Dangerous. Fatal.

And I whispered to myself, voice shaking but strong enough to feel real: "It's time to go home (and hope Kareem forgets about me quick).

CHAPTER
17

Back to Atlanta, Bigger Than Ever

The wheels hit the runway with a screech that rattled through my chest. I gripped the armrest, heart racing like it always did when I touched back down in the States. Home. But not the home I left.

The door of the jet swung open, and Atlanta's humid air wrapped around me thick and sticky. It wasn't Dubai's dry desert breeze. This was sweat-on-your-skin, mosquito-buzzing, barbecue-smelling Atlanta air. And for the first time in months, I inhaled it like medicine.

Parked right at the bottom of the stairs was my prize, the black Rolls Royce Phantom gleaming under the Georgia sun. Fresh off the ship from Dubai, shipped straight from Kareem's pocket to mine. The chrome grill winked at me like it already knew I was the baddest bitch in the city.

Behind it, moving trucks lined up, stacked with crates of designer: Chanel, Dior, Balmain, Louis. Bags and boxes stuffed with jewelry, gowns, and shit I hadn't even worn yet. My new life packed tighter than dope in a brick.

I walked down the stairs slow, heels clicking against the metal like a countdown. The driver opened the door for me, bowing slightly. My reflection hit me in the tinted glass: blonde bob wig, diamond choker snug on my neck, shades big enough to block the world.

Jasmine from Memphis was dead. Phantum was all that was left.

They were waiting.

Donna stood bold in the Rolls' shadow, thick thighs stuffed into some too-tight Fashion Nova, nails long enough to poke an eye out. "Damn, bitch," she hollered, grinning wide. "You done leveled the fuck up!"

I laughed, hugging her tight, the familiar smell of cocoa butter and weed wrapping around me. Tika was quieter, arms crossed, eyes scanning the boxes stacked high. She gave me a quick hug, but her face stayed flat.

"All this?" she asked, lips pursed. "You sure it's safe bringing this kinda attention back here? Atlanta ain't Dubai."

I slid my shades down just enough to lock eyes with her. "Safe ain't never been part of my plan, Tika. Big risk, big reward. You know that."

Donna cackled, fanning herself. "Shit, I'm just tryna ride in that Rolls. Let these Atlanta niggas see us pull up looking like a million dollars."

I smirked, sliding into the backseat, letting the leather swallow me whole. "Correction, baby. Thirty-five million in cash, ten in crypto. Let's get the numbers right."

Donna screamed, smacking my thigh. "Bitch, you rich rich!"

Tika shook her head, sliding in beside me, her tone low. "Rich don't mean safe, Jas. Money bring snakes. You know that better than anybody."

I leaned back, the city skyline flickering outside as we rolled. "And that's why I wear the mask. Let 'em guess. Let 'em whisper. They'll never see me coming."

The first night back, I had to make it loud. Couldn't creep into the city like I was scared. If I wanted Atlanta to know Phantum was home, I had to let the streets hear me before they even saw me.

The black Rolls Royce glided down Peachtree like it owned the asphalt. Donna hung half out the window, hair flying, nails flashing in the streetlights. "Y'all see us?" she screamed at a group of dudes on the corner, their jaws dropping. "Phantum back, bitches!"

I laughed, sipping champagne from the backseat, shades still on even though it was midnight. Tika sat stiff, eyes darting around like she was scanning for trouble.

"This too much attention," she muttered. "Niggas watching. You don't know who jealous, who plotting."

I smirked, lips curling. "Tika, jealousy just free promotion. Let 'em watch. That's how they know they can't touch me."

Hottest club in the city, people waiting outside everywhere, and all eyes peeped the Rolls. I stepped out slow, diamonds on my neck catching every light, gown hugging my hips like it was painted on. Gasps rippled through the line — some whispers of "Who dat?" mixed with "Ain't that Phantum?"

The crowd parted for us like Moses at the Red Sea. I walked through with Donna and Tika flanking me, eyes following every step.

At the VIP section, bottles lined the table before I even sat down. Ace of Spades, Henny, sparklers shooting like fireworks. Donna was already on the couch, dancing, pouring liquor straight into her mouth, screaming over the music.

Tika sat close, voice sharp in my ear. "This what you missed? Flashy shit? Attention like a target on your back?"

I leaned in, smirking, my lips brushing her ear. "I didn't miss it. I came back to remind 'em who I am."

But even in the noise, even in the glow of money and lights, my paranoia hummed. Every time a man lingered too long near the section, every time a camera phone tilted my way, my stomach tightened.

In my head, I could still see Kareem's calm face in that basement. Still hear the screams. Still smell the blood.

I sipped my drink, mask tight, smile wide. Nobody in here would ever know I was shaking inside. But deep down, I whispered to myself: "Play the game, but don't get caught slippin'. Not here. Not now."

My condo was calm when Tika slid in, still smelling like the club, wig tilted from all that bass shaking her head. She kicked her heels off by the door, dropped her bag on the couch, and flopped down next to me.

Stacks of cash stared at us from the dining table, jewels glittering under the soft lights. For a minute, we just sat in the silence, the weight of it all pressing down.

I sighed, rubbing my temples. "Tika, I ain't gon' lie to you. I'm tired."

She looked at me sideways. "Tired? Girl, you sittin' on millions. What the hell you tired of?"

"The game," I said, voice low. "The lies, the licks, the niggas who think they own me. I got enough to retire right now, disappear if I want. Part of me...part of me wanna just walk away."

Tika's jaw dropped. "Phantum? Retire? Stop playin'."

I smirked, sipping from my glass. "Dead serious. Me and you always talked about it, remember? Miami. Just us, no stress. Sand under our feet, no niggas blowing up our phones. Just peace for once."

For a second, her face softened. "Damn... you really mean that?"

I nodded. "I think it's time."

She leaned in close, voice dropping to a whisper. "Then you need to hear what the streets been saying."

My stomach tightened. "What streets saying now?"

Tika bit her lip, eyes darting to the window like somebody might be listening. "They saying that hit you barely walked away from? That wasn't no random. Word is, Donna lined that shit up."

The glass in my hand froze halfway to my lips. "What?"

"She was too loud, too messy. Niggas say she wanted your spot, your shine. Used the wrong people, and it backfired. But her name all in the whispers, Jas. All in it."

My heart pounded, heat rushing to my face. Donna. My so-called road dog. My partner in crime. Setting me up? I wondered at the time it happened but had decided she was straight.

For a second, I wanted to storm out, find her, handle it Memphis-style right then. But I forced myself to breathe. To think.

"Alright," I said finally, jaw tight. "Then fuck it. We go to Miami like we planned. Just me and you, Tika. No Donna. Time to clear my head, figure out my next move."

Tika nodded, relief flickering in her eyes.
"Yeah, Miami. Just us. About time we did
something for ourselves."
I stood, grabbing my phone, already pulling up
flights. My chest was hot with anger, but my
face stayed cool.

"Yeah," I whispered. "Miami. But when I get
back? Donna gon' learn what happens when
you put my name in dirt."

CHAPTER

18

Miami Moves

The second the jet door opened, Miami smacked me in the face like a warm, wet hand. Thick air smelling like ocean salt, weed smoke, and Cuban food. It wasn't the dry heat of Dubai; it wasn't the grit of Atlanta. This was a whole different type of playground.

"Damn," Tika said, fanning herself as we walked down the steps. "This shit feel like somebody put a blanket over the whole city."

I laughed, slipping my shades down. "Girl, this the type of heat that make clothes optional. Watch how fast Miami gon' have us half-naked."

The driver was waiting with the keys to a Rolls Cullinan, white on white, spinning slow in the sun. We slid in, leather seats soft as butter, and rode through the city with palm trees swaying overhead. Ocean Drive was alive — neon signs, music blasting, ass cheeks bouncing on every corner. Foreign cars lined the streets: Lambos revving, Maybachs creeping, Bentleys shining.

When we got to the penthouse suite I'd rented, Tika damn near fell out when she saw the view.

Floor-to-ceiling windows stretched over South Beach, the ocean glistening blue under the sun, yachts dotting the water like floating mansions.

"Bitchhhh!" Tika screamed, running to the window. "Look at this shit! Jas, we ain't never leaving!"

I tossed a Dior bag on the couch. "We could stay if you dress right. This Miami. You can't step out lookin' regular."

She turned, eyes wide. "Wait...what's this?"

I smirked. "Open it."

Tika pulled out a Dior dress, silky and black with straps thin as shoelaces. She held it up against her body, gasping. "Girl...this Dior? You serious?"

I nodded, lighting a blunt. "First designer with your name on it. You been ridin' with me too long to still be wearin' Fashion Nova."

185

She pressed it to her chest, eyes shining. "I swear to God, I'ma cry. I always told you I wanted my first real bag, my first designer piece, to come from my best friend. And here you go, outdoing yourself."

"Don't cry, bitch," I teased, blowing smoke. "Just put that shit on and shut the city down with me tonight."

By nightfall, we were ready.

Tika stepped out the bathroom first, Dior hugging her curves like it was painted on. The dress shimmered under the light, every step making her thighs clap, her cleavage sitting so high it looked like she was serving them on a platter. She twirled, laughing. "How the fuck I look, Jas?"

I sat on the edge of the bed, rolling up another blunt, giving her a slow once-over. "Bitch, you look like trouble. Miami ain't ready."

Then it was my turn. Chanel bikini top under a silk skirt slit to my hip, every step flashing thigh and ass cheek. My tits sat perky, damn near spilling out the top, nipples brushing the silk with every breath. I oiled up my skin so it glowed golden under the lights, diamonds heavy around my neck, catching sparks with every move.

When we walked out the penthouse, the valet boy damn near dropped his keys staring.

"Yeah, keep looking, lil' nigga," I said, sliding my shades on. "We just getting started."

The Rolls pulled up slow, purring like a beast. South Beach was lit: girls half-naked in thong bikinis, asses shaking on scooters, music blasting from cars crawling down the strip. Men shouted, whistled, some tryna flag us down like we was celebrities.

"Damn, Jas," Tika said, leaning back in the seat. "We ain't even at the club yet, and they treatin' us like we famous."

I grinned, lipstick glowing under the neon. "That's 'cause we are. Miami just ain't caught up yet."

We pulled up to a club where the line wrapped around the block. Phones shot up as soon as the Rolls stopped, flashes popping like fireworks.

The promoter ran to the door, sweat dripping down his bald head. "Phantum! Welcome to Miami, baby. You and your girl ain't waiting for shit. Come on."

Inside, the club was wild — bass shaking the floor, lights slicing through smoke, bodies grinding everywhere.

Tika laughed loud, throwing her arms up. "Miami lit as fuck!"

I adjusted my shades, tits bouncing with every step, diamonds flashing, ass swaying like it had its own beat. Every set of eyes followed us. Some whispered my name. Others just stared like they were starving.

That's when I saw them.

A matte-black Lamborghini slid to a stop outside the club, doors lifting slow. Two brothers stepped out, and the whole block shifted.

The first was tall, dark-skinned, shoulders wide, Cartier shades hiding his eyes, diamond chain thick as a python. The second wore a silk shirt unbuttoned to his navel, abs gleaming in the neon, Rolex sparkling every time he raised his hand.

They didn't rush. They didn't have to. People moved out of their way. And the second their eyes locked on us, I knew Miami was about to get dangerous.

The crowd parted like they always do when big money walks in — but this time it wasn't chains clanking or bottles spraying that did it. It was quiet. They walked smooth, not a flash in sight. No sparklers, no entourage, no screaming women trailing behind them, two men who carried themselves like the street was theirs, and they didn't have to say a word about it.

The taller one wore a plain black tee that fit snug across his chest, Cartier frames sitting low on his nose. No giant chain, just a slim watch that whispered money instead of screaming it. The younger one had on a silk shirt, loose, half unbuttoned, skin glowing under the neon. His smile was lazy, but his eyes sharp, scanning everything without looking pressed.

I caught myself staring. Not at the cars or the clothes — at the calm.

"Damn," Tika muttered in my ear, sipping her drink. "Why they look like they know everything and ain't worried about shit?"

I smirked, eyes still locked. "That's exactly why I like it."

They didn't rush to us. Didn't call out. Didn't send a bottle or flash a card. They just moved through the crowd slow, steady, like the whole club was background noise.

When they reached our section, the taller one nodded once. "Evening." His voice was deep, smooth, carrying over the bass without him raising it.

Donna would've giggled. Other girls might've jumped to flirt. I leaned back in my seat, one eyebrow raised. "Evening."

The younger one smiled, hands in his pockets, eyes flicking from me to Tika. "You're not from here."

"Depends who's asking," I shot back.

He chuckled, the sound low, easy. "Somebody who noticed the whole room watching you, but you only watching us."

That made me pause. Then I laughed, soft but real. "Fair enough."

We talked. Not about money, not about cars, not about bullshit. They asked me about Memphis, about Atlanta, about the kind of music I liked, what I thought of Miami so far.

And the way they listened? No phone in hand, no eyes drifting. Just focus. Presence.

Most men I dealt with couldn't go five minutes without bragging about what they owned or what they spent. These two didn't say shit about money. And that silence was louder than any chain or car.

Tika was beaming, sipping heavy, but I sat there studying them, something hot curling inside me.

For the first time in a long time, I wasn't thinking about a lick. I wasn't thinking about setting nobody up. I just wanted to know who the fuck these two were and why they moved like they owned the night without touching it.

The taller one finally pulled his shades off, sliding them into his pocket. His eyes were sharp, steady, like he'd already read the whole room twice and didn't need to look again. He held out his hand, no rush, no pressure.

"Diego," he said simply. His voice was deep, slow, carrying that Cuban lilt under the smoothness.

I slipped my hand into his, warm and firm. "Phantum," I said, mask tight.

The younger one leaned against the rail, silk shirt swaying with the bass, smile easy but not careless. "And I'm Mateo," he added, his accent softer, rolling off his tongue like he'd grown up switching between Spanish at home and English in the streets.

Tika giggled, brushing her braids back. "Diego and Mateo, huh? Y'all sound like y'all supposed to be on a yacht somewhere, not in this sweaty-ass club."

Mateo chuckled, tilting his head. "Maybe we just wanted to see what Miami had to offer tonight." His eyes slid back to me. "Looks like we found it."

Up close, it was clearer: Diego carried himself like the type who thought ten moves ahead, calm, unreadable. Broad shoulders under that plain black tee, arms cut but not exaggerated, skin the color of warm bronze.

Mateo was leaner, smoother, his curls pulled back tight, gold stud in his ear catching the light. His smile was mischievous, but his eyes stayed sharp, scanning, clocking everything without looking pressed.

They weren't trying to impress us with chains or bottles. They weren't raising their voices over the music. They just...were.

And that was enough.

I felt something twist in my chest, something I wasn't used to. Interest. Real interest.

Not in their wallets. Not in a setup. But in them.

Diego leaned closer, his cologne hitting — subtle, wood and spice, nothing loud. "You two seem out of place here," he said calmly.

"Out of place?" I raised an eyebrow.

He nodded once. "Too polished for this crowd. Too calm. Like you don't belong in noise."

That hit. I smirked, tilting my head. "And where we supposed to belong, then?"

Mateo slid his hands deeper in his pockets, smile tugging at his lips. "Somewhere quieter. Somewhere better." He glanced at Diego, then back at me. "Our place. Tomorrow. Pool. Dinner. Music that don't hurt your ears."

Tika's eyes lit up. "Nigga, say less. We there."

I chuckled, sipping my drink slow, but inside, my pulse jumped. I wasn't used to men like this. They weren't chasing. They were inviting. And somehow, that was harder to resist.

The phone buzzed again, then went quiet. CJ's name faded from the screen, but the weight of it sat heavy in my chest.

Tika slid closer, lowering her voice. "You know you gotta call his lawyer back, right? That lady don't play about her schedule."

I sighed, rubbing my temples. "Yeah, I know. I been dodging it."

"Jas," she said firmly, "you put money into that case. Don't let all this," she waved her hand around the villa, the pool, the champagne, the brothers lounging like gods, "don't let this make you forget. We still got business back home. Donna still out there, too."

Her words snapped me back. Miami was beautiful. Diego and Mateo were...tempting. But I had unfinished blood in Atlanta.

I leaned back, exhaling smoke from my blunt. "Yeah. You right. We gon' enjoy this for now, but soon as we touch down back home, I'ma handle Donna. Manage CJ's lawyer. Then, when it's clean? We come back."

Tika winked, clinking her glass against mine. "Bet. Miami gon' be here. Them brothers gon' be here too. Regulate home first."

I nodded, eyes drifting to Diego across the pool, his calm gaze locking on mine. My pulse jumped, but my mind sharpened.

Business first. Always business first.

CHAPTER

19

The Brothers' Empire

The lobby didn't scream money; it whispered it. Cool air rolled across marble, a living wall of jade plants drank the morning light, and a single chrome plaque on the stone read:

ALVAREZ TECHNOLOGIES

No tagline. No hype line about "changing the world." Just a name that knew you'd google it later.

The security guard recognized Diego with a nod, then glanced at me and Tika with that careful curiosity men get when they're not sure if you're famous or just look like trouble. Diego passed a black card across the glass; the turnstile clicked. Mateo bumped my shoulder, playful.

"First time in a place where the quiet's louder than the music?" he asked.

I smirked. "I like rooms that don't need to shout."

Tika leaned into me, eyes wide at the ceilings. "Girl, this look like somewhere rent got commas."

We stepped into a private elevator — mirror-polished steel, no button panel, just a faint chime when Diego tapped his phone. "Forty," he said. The doors closed, and we rose like the building was breathing us in.

"Alvarez Technologies is... what?" I asked. "I saw coders downstairs. Looked like NASA with better shoes." Mateo's smile tugged. "We build decision engines. AI that helps big companies stop bleeding money. Logistics. Risk. Security. A few government contracts we don't talk about at brunch."

"'Decision engines'?" Tika echoed, suspicious and impressed at the same time. "That sound like y'all telling people what to do."

"In a way," Diego said. "We predict. They decide. We just...make the fog thinner."

The elevator opened on glass and light. An entire floor of clean lines and quiet focus: rows of engineers with headphones, a war-room wall of dashboards pulsing in color, clusters of whiteboards covered in arrows and Greek letters. A woman in a slate suit peeled toward us, tablet in hand.

"Morning," she said, warmth sliding under crisp professionalism. "Liana, COO. You must be Jasmine. Tika." Firm handshake, clear eye contact. "We don't get many tours. But my brothers insisted."

I clocked the "my brothers" and tucked it away. Family ran this place, not founders performing for venture capitalists.

Liana gestured to a display wall. "This is Aurelia, our core platform. Computer vision for ports and yards, predictive models for supply chains, anomaly detection for payments. If something breaks or someone cheats, Aurelia sees it first." She flicked her wrist; on screen, containers glided across a digital port, cranes moving like ballerinas. Little flags popped up — yellow, then red — where delays or fraud likely hid.

"Who buys that?" I asked.

"Everyone who bleeds," Diego said. "Retailers. Insurers. Carriers. Ministries. If a late shipment can lose you eight figures, you take prevention personally."

"And y'all get paid how?" Tika said, blunt as always.

"Subscription for the software," Liana said, unfazed. "Upside fees when our models outperform human benchmarks. Some contracts include revenue-share if we cut losses past a threshold."

Mateo shrugged. "Save someone fifty million, they don't mind paying you five."

We moved past a glassed-in lab where two small robot arms fed parts into bins while a camera above them sorted defects in real time. A young engineer raised a hand at Mateo like a kid proud of a science fair project.

"Edge model's down to six milliseconds inference," he called. "Sub-seven across the line."

"Bueno," Mateo said. "Ship it."

He caught my look. "Milliseconds matter when you stop theft or fires or brakes failing at seventy miles an hour. Not glamorous, just necessary."

"Necessary makes money," Diego added. "Glamour spends it."

We drifted to a softer space with walnut shelves and a black-and-white photo of a Havana street pinned beside one of Overtown in the seventies. On a side table: a faded baseball, a humidor, a rosary. The brothers' past and present in a still life.

"Your last name not just for the sign," I said.

Diego's gaze touched the photos. "Our father ran stevedore gangs—loading ships—after he came from Cuba. Our mother taught math. We wrote our first app at nineteen in a one-bedroom off 8th Street with a view of a brick wall. Sold it. Didn't buy cars." He nodded to the skyline. "Bought dirt. Brickell when it was cheap. Wynwood when it was warehouses. Then we bought time—engineers, talent, patents."

"And now?" Tika said, brows up.

Mateo's voice stayed casual. "Now we're worth around one-five."

"Billion," Liana added, dry, as if she were correcting a rounding error.

Tika's jaw actually dropped. "With a B? Boy..."

I nudged her and kept my face smooth, pulse kicking but mask unbroken. I'd been around rich, loud men. These were rich, quiet men. Different species.

We crossed to another glass room where a wall showed a U.S. map flecked with green dots springing to life.

"ACP," Diego said. "Alvarez Capital Properties. We hold and manage. Class-A multifamily in Orlando and Miami; medical office in Broward; logistics parks outside Savannah and Lakeland. We use leverage when it's cheap; trade out when cap rates lie. Nothing heroic. Just discipline."

"Patient money," Mateo said. "We like deals that look boring on social media and obscene on spreadsheets."

I let myself smile. "Y'all allergic to flex, huh?"

Diego's mouth ticked. "Flex is cost. Attention is cost. We spend on assets."

Liana's tablet buzzed; she stepped away, murmuring to someone about a "Gulf tender" and "final diligence."

I turned back to the brothers. "So why show me this? I'm not a VC. I don't code."

"We didn't bring you to code," Mateo said, head tilted. "We brought you to see our language. We don't need models for attention. We build engines that last."

Diego's eyes held mine. "You read rooms better than most read books. We respect that. You don't look impressed. That's rare."

"I'm impressed," I said. "I just don't clap where I pray."

A corner of his mouth lifted. "Good."

We moved again—into a dim conference room where the city floated beneath us like a map of stars. Liana returned and slid a folder across the table. A simple cover: Partnership Overview.

"No NDAs yet," she said. "Just context. We're rolling out a private family office fund, quiet co-investments alongside us in logistics and data centers. We've turned down influencers, ballplayers, even a senator's nephew. But..." Her eyes flicked from Diego to me. "We're exploring a brand of discretion. Appear nowhere. But be everywhere."

Mateo laced his fingers. "We'd want to understand your world. Not the Instagram version. The real one."

My phone buzzed in my purse—just once—a reminder ping to call the lawyer's office I'd bankrolled for CJ. I let the vibration finish, a thread pulling me back to Atlanta even as Miami laid itself at my feet.

Tika caught it too; her knee brushed mine under the table. Don't forget. Her look said everything.

Mateo turned his palm up, easy. "You don't have to answer now."

"We don't want you to," Diego said. "We don't move fast. We move right."

"Give me your diligence list," I said. "I'll give you mine."

Diego looked...pleased. "Reciprocity. Good."

Liana slid a single page my way. Three lines. Background. Conflicts. Intent.

"You can keep the paper," she said. "We prefer truth to signatures."

Tika exhaled a whisper. "These folks different."

I closed the folder, stood, and walked to the glass. The bay glittered. Cargo ships in the distance crawled toward cranes that looked like praying mantises. Somewhere in those tiny movements, someone was saving or losing millions—depending on what an engine predicted and who listened.

Behind me, chairs shifted, low voices traded in Spanish, "tranquila," "proceso," "limpio." Calm. Process. Clean.

I turned back. "Tomorrow I've got calls. Back in Atlanta, I got things to close. Messes to clean."

Diego nodded once. "Handle home."

Mateo's smile softened. "Miami won't move. We've held it this long."

I reached for Tika's hand. "We'll circle back."

"Noted," Liana said.

We walked to the elevator. As the doors slid, Diego's reflection aligned with mine in the mirrored steel. Two silhouettes that didn't need noise to know their own weight.

In my bag, the phone buzzed again—CJ's lawyer texted saying she had updates as requested. That issue was moved to the back burner of my mind, though; Donna's name kept rising in my mind like a storm cloud over Peachtree.

I glanced back at Diego and Mateo through the narrowing slit of the elevator doors. No flex. No push. Just patience.

"Yeah," I said, as the doors sealed us in. "I think it will."

Their villa was tranquil that night. Pool lights glowed blue, casting ripples on the glass walls. Diego sat at the long dining table, a glass of red wine in hand, reading something on his tablet. Mateo leaned back in the chair across from me, rolling a cigar between his fingers. Tika sat stiff at my side, twisting her braids like she was working up the nerve to speak.

I broke the silence. "There's something I need to tell y'all," I said, my voice low but sharp.

Diego didn't look up right away. When he did, his eyes were steady, patient. "Go ahead."

"It's about a woman. Somebody close. Somebody who almost got me killed."

Mateo flicked the cigar, still calm. "Name?"

I hesitated. Saying it out loud made it real. "Donna."

Tika slammed her palm against the table. "That bitch set Jas up! Streets been whispering it since we got back. She lined the hit, thinking Jas wouldn't make it out alive. I swear to God, if I ever see her..."

"Breathe," Diego cut her off, his tone like steel wrapped in velvet. She shut her mouth instantly.

I leaned forward, palms flat on the table. "She was supposed to be my dog. My rider. I fed her, dressed her. Then she got greedy. Tried to take me out."

Mateo studied me, that lazy smile gone. "What do you want?"

"I want her gone," I said, no hesitation.

Diego set the wine glass down, folded his hands. "Then she will be gone."

Tika blinked. "Just like that?"

He nodded once. "Just like that. We don't let betrayal breathe. Not in our family. Not in our circle. Someone touches what's ours, they don't get second chances."

Mateo lit the cigar finally, smoke curling between us. His eyes locked on mine. "We'll make it clean. No mess. Nobody will tie it back to you. All you'll have to do...is live like she never existed."

For the first time, I felt a chill run down my spine. Not fear. Respect.

Diego leaned back. "We'll set a stage. A party. Fake flyer, fake invite. Somewhere she thinks she'll shine. She'll come easy — people like her always do. And when she walks in..." He shrugged. "She won't walk back out."

Tika's mouth hung open. "Y'all serious?"

Diego's gaze cut sharp. "Do we look like men who waste words?"

Mateo blew smoke, smirk curling. "Welcome to our world, Jas. You don't have to dirty your hands. But if you want to watch...that can be arranged."

I sat back, heart pounding steady, face unreadable. Inside, I wanted to smile. Not because I loved the idea of blood — but because for the first time, I wasn't the one carrying it all on my back.

"Set it up," I said. "I'll be there."

Diego nodded once, final. "It's done."

CHAPTER

20

Ghosts & Chains

The sun was just rising over Biscayne Bay when I slipped out of the villa. Diego was still asleep, his arm heavy across my waist, his scent still on my skin. For a moment, I thought about staying — curling back into that warmth, letting Miami swallow me whole.

But CJ's name was buzzing in my head like an alarm I couldn't shut off.

By noon, I was back on a plane, Tika beside me, both of us quiet as the jet cut through clouds. Miami glittered smaller and smaller beneath us until it was nothing but blue water. Ahead was Atlanta — grit, ghosts, and a lawyer waiting with news I wasn't sure I wanted to hear.

Tika finally broke the silence. "You ready for this?"

I stared out the window, sunglasses hiding my eyes. "Don't matter if I'm ready. It's here."

Downtown Atlanta hit different after Miami. No palm trees, no ocean breeze. Just heat rising off cracked sidewalks, sirens in the distance, and skyscrapers that looked more tired than powerful.

We stepped into the law office — leather chairs, cold AC, the smell of old books and fresh coffee. A receptionist with stiff curls led us back to a glass-walled conference room where Attorney Graves sat waiting.

She was a sharp Black woman in a navy suit, glasses perched on her nose, papers stacked neat in front of her. Her eyes lifted as we walked in, and for once, I felt like a little girl again, caught sneaking into grown folks' business.

"Ms. Jasmine," Graves said, standing to shake my hand. Her grip was firm. "And you must be Tika."

Tika nodded, sitting down quick. I stayed standing a second longer, adjusting my shades, then finally sat across from the lawyer.

"You said you had updates," I said flatly. My voice was steady, but my stomach twisted.

Graves folded her hands on the table. "Yes. About Chris Clark's case."

My chest tightened hearing his name out loud.

She continued. "We've filed the appeal. The parole board has reviewed his record, and there are signs they may be open to a release hearing. But..."

Always a damn but.

"But," she said, "they'll need letters. Proof of stable housing, financial backing, and community support. If we can show he has a safety net, a future outside prison, then we have a real shot."

I swallowed, jaw tight. "And if not?"

Her eyes held mine. "Then he stays inside."

Graves slid a folder across the table. Inside: forms, checklists, blank spaces waiting for promises. "Stable housing. Employment plan. Financial support," she said, tapping each line with a manicured nail. "These aren't optional. Without them, the board won't even consider him."

I stared at the papers, my reflection bent across the glossy sheet. Stable housing? I had condos, penthouses, villas. Employment? CJ wasn't no nine-to-five man. Financial support? I had more money than some small nations.

The problem wasn't the resources. It was me.

Tika leaned over, skimming the list. "This ain't nothing, Jas. You can write all this up tomorrow. Drop a couple bank statements, sign some papers. They'll be lettin' CJ out by summer."

I shot her a look. "You think it's that easy?"

She frowned. "It is that easy. You got the bread. You got the spots. You got the name. The real question is..." she paused, her voice low, "...do you even want him out?"

The room went still. Even Graves glanced at me over her glasses, waiting.

Heat flared in my chest. "Don't play with me, Ti. Of course I want him out."

"Do you?" she pushed. "You was laid up in Miami like a queen, dripping in Dior, fucking with billionaires. And now you back here ready to promise a whole life for a man who been locked twenty years? A man who broke you before he ever built you?"

"Watch your mouth," I snapped, slamming the folder shut.

Tika leaned back, arms crossed. "I'm just saying, Jas. Don't mix loyalty with love. They don't always mean the same thing."

My pulse thundered in my ears. CJ's face flashed in my mind — young, sharp, gold chain glinting in the sun. Then Diego's face overlapped it — calm, unreadable, steady even with blood still warm on his hands.

Two men. Two worlds. And me stuck between them.

Graves cleared her throat. "Ms. Jasmine, I don't know your personal history, and frankly, it's not my business. What I do know is the parole board only cares about paper. If you want Chris out, this is the price."

She tapped the folder again.

"Chains," I whispered under my breath. Paper chains. That's all it came down to.

The glass doors of Graves' office slammed behind me harder than I meant. Atlanta air smacked me in the face — thick, hot, smelling like exhaust and fried food. Nothing like Miami's breeze. Nothing like Diego's sheets.

I stopped on the sidewalk, folder in my hand, palms sweating against the paper.

Tika jogged up beside me, heels clicking. "Jas, slow down."

I spun on her, my shades barely hiding the fire in my eyes. "You really had to come at me like that in there?"

She threw her hands up. "I ain't say nothing that wasn't true. You still in love with a nigga sitting in a cell while you got billionaires buying you wine and silk. Which side you really on, Jas?"

My chest rose, hot. "Don't act like you know my heart."

"I don't gotta know it," she snapped. "I see it. You been different since Miami. Different since him." She didn't even have to say Diego's name — I felt it in the pause.

I turned away, swallowing hard, staring at the cars rolling by. For a second, I wanted to break. To tell her how torn I felt. How Diego's calm made me feel safe in ways CJ's chaos never did. How CJ's ghost still whispered in my ear even when Diego's hands were on my skin.

Instead, I pulled out my phone.

The prison number stared back at me. I hadn't answered in Miami. But I couldn't run forever.

I hit dial.

The line clicked. Static. Then his voice.

"Jas?" CJ sounded the same — older, rougher, but still that same low tone that used to melt me.

My throat closed. "Yeah. It's me."

Silence stretched. Then he chuckled, low. "Thought you forgot about me. Left me in here to rot."

"I ain't forget," I whispered. My hand shook, gripping the phone like it might slip. "I been working. Hired a lawyer. She thinks we got a shot."

Another pause. Then softer: "Damn, baby. You really still riding for me after all this time?"

Tika stood beside me, arms crossed, rolling her eyes like she wanted to snatch the phone and hang it up. But I couldn't.

Because hearing his voice? It pulled me back to being thirteen on a summer night, his chain glinting, his hand warm on my thigh, his words teaching me how to survive.

I closed my eyes, whispering so low Tika couldn't hear: "I'll always ride for you, CJ." But deep down, I wondered if I was lying.

The prison line hummed, CJ's voice low and heavy in my ear. "Jas, you know what this mean, right? If the board see me got a home, got money, got love waiting... that's freedom. That's us again."

His words dripped like syrup, sweet and sticky, hard to shake off.

"I'll set it up," I said, barely above a whisper. "Condos, cash, whatever they need. I got you."

CJ chuckled, the sound wrapping around me like a rope. "That's my girl."

The call clicked dead, but the echo of his voice clung to me.

Outside, Tika lit a cigarette, blowing smoke hard. "Jas, you sound like a damn fool." My jaw was clenched and she kept on even when I threw my hand in her face to shut her up.

"I'ma say it," she snapped. "That man had you on your knees when you was barely a teenager. He ran your heart, ran your mind, and you still letting him. You don't even hear yourself, do you?"

I shoved the folder against her chest. "You don't know what we got. CJ is... he's deeper than some old fling. He's part of me."

Tika rolled her eyes. "Part of you or controlling you?"

My voice cracked, sharp but soft. "Both."

For a second, she just stared at me, like she didn't recognize who she was looking at anymore. Then she muttered, "Do you, Jas. But don't say I ain't warn you."

I turned away, my pulse pounding, CJ's voice still whispering in my ear like I'd never hung up.

That night, back in the condo, I lay in bed with the folder on my lap, staring at the blank letterhead Graves had given me.

Stable housing. Financial proof. Letters of support. All it would take was a few signatures, a few promises — and CJ could walk free.

Diego's touch was still fresh on my skin from Miami. His steadiness, his calm power. And yet...here I was, smiling like a teenager every time CJ's voice replayed in my head.

My phone buzzed. Miami number. Diego. I let it ring out.

Instead, I pulled out a pen, touched it to the paper, and started writing like my heart was on trial.

Chris Clark is more than an inmate. He is a man who has a home waiting. He is a man with love waiting. He is a man with a future.

The words blurred as tears pricked my eyes, but I kept writing. Because no matter how high I climbed, no matter how much I built, CJ was my weak spot.

CHAPTER

21

Paper Crown

The metal doors clanged shut behind me like the past locking me in again. That smell hit me before anything else — bleach, sweat, and something stale, like time had been sitting in here too long and rotted.

It'd been years since I stepped foot in this place. I used to swear I'd never come back. But here I was, sliding my ID across bulletproof glass, signing my name like I was clocking into old trauma.

The waiting room buzzed with women who looked like me in different fonts — girlfriends, baby mamas, wives, sisters, daughters. All of us with bags under our eyes and hearts that refused to quit. Some held babies. Some held bibles. I held my composure like it was the last luxury item I owned.

The guard waved me through. My heels clicked too loud down the hallway, echoing off cinderblock like a soundtrack. When I stepped into the visitation room, it was more of the same: rows of plastic chairs, thick glass, black phones hanging from hooks, a line of men already waiting in state greens and oranges.

And then I saw him.

CJ.

Even under fluorescent lights, even in that faded green, he still carried himself like he owned everything he could see. Hair cut low, shoulders broader now, jaw tighter from grinding through years. When his eyes found mine, that old smirk spread across his face like he'd been practicing it for me in the mirror this whole time.

"Damn," he mouthed through the glass, shaking his head slow. "Jas."

My heart did this stupid little flip I wish I could blame on anything but him. I swallowed, slid into the chair, and picked up the phone, fingers trembling more than I wanted to admit.

"Look at you," he said, his voice filling my ear like no time had passed. "Shit. You ain't aged a day. Got finer though. You glowin'."

I rolled my eyes, trying to keep it cute. "You flatterin' me from behind bulletproof glass, CJ. That don't count."

"Nah, I'm speakin' facts." His gaze moved over me through the glass, hunger and pride both there. "You walked in here like you runnin' the whole damn world. You got that queen shit now. But I can still see my Jas in there."

My throat tightened. "Your Jas, huh?"

"Always been mine," he said, smooth as ever. "Don't matter how far you ran, who you wit'... I can still feel you."

The way he said it — like everybody else I'd ever been with was just background noise — I hated what it did to me. My body remembered him faster than my mind did. That was always the danger.

"CJ..." I shook my head, tried to steady my voice. "It's been twenty years. You in here. I'm out there. Life changed."

He leaned closer, eyes locked on mine, voice dropping lower. "Life changed, but feelings don't. You think I ain't thought about you every night I laid in that cell? You think I ain't planned what we gon' do when I walk out? Jas, we still got a story to finish."

I wanted to say no. Wanted to say the story was over, credits rolled, we buried that shit behind Capitol Homes. Instead, what came out was soft, almost a whisper.

"You still talk like you runnin' shit."

His grin widened. "'Cause I am. You just forgot for a minute. But it's cool. I'ma remind you."

Silence stretched between us, heavy and loud. The room buzzed with other people's mess, but it felt like just me and him trapped in our own old movie. Finally, I swallowed and said the thing I came here to say. "I'm getting you out."

His eyes sharpened. "What?"

"The lawyer said we got a shot," I told him. "Good behavior, time served, support on the outside. I'm lining everything up. I'm gonna do whatever it takes."

For the first time, the slickness slipped off his face. His confidence cracked and something raw peeked through. His eyes got glossy and he had to look down for a second before he met my stare again.

"You serious?" he asked.

"Yeah," I said, voice steady now. "Dead serious."

He closed his eyes, exhaled slow, nodded like he was accepting something holy. "That's why you mine, Jas. Nobody else could hold me down like you. Nobody."

The guard barked from the corner. "Time's up!"

My body jolted, but my hand didn't move. Neither did his. CJ pressed his palm flat against the glass, eyes locked on mine.

"Don't you let go this time," he said, voice rough now. "Don't you dare."

My hand lifted before I could stop it, pressing against the cold glass, lining up with his. For a second, it felt like the past and present were both touching — young us, dumb us, grown us, broken us — all at once.

The guard shouted again. Chairs scraped. Women sniffled. Doors buzzed. I dropped the phone back into its cradle and forced myself to stand.

I walked out with my pulse racing, lips tingling, body weak like I was seventeen again sneaking kisses in stairwells.

CJ still had me. And I hated how much I loved it.

When those doors slid open and that hot sun slapped my face, it felt wrong that the world was just...regular. Cars honking. Birds chirping. Somebody arguing on speakerphone in the parking lot like life wasn't shifting under my feet.

Tika was posted up on the hood of my Range, gum popping, arms crossed, attitude ready. Soon as she clocked my face, she groaned.

"Girl. You fuckin' smiling," she said, sliding off the hood. "After all that? You actually smiling."

I tugged my shades down to cover my eyes. "You dramatic."

"He ain't even touch you and you walking out here like you just got some dick," she said, loud as hell. "Goddamn, Jas. What is it about that man?"

I brushed past her and hit the unlock. "You wouldn't understand."

She grabbed the door, stopping me from closing it. "Nah. Make me understand." I sighed, got in anyway, and let her stomp around to the passenger side. She slammed the door like she was tryna shake sense into me through the frame.

We pulled off and rode in silence for a minute. My head was loud. My chest louder. CJ's voice still echoing, still wrapping around me like smoke.

By the time we hit downtown, Tika folded her arms tight and let it out. "What the fuck was that in there?"

I kept my eyes on the road. "What you talkin' about?"

"What I'm talkin' about is you walked in that prison bossed up, queen energy all over you... and walked out lookin' like his lil girlfriend from back in the day," she snapped. "You let him pull you right back like twenty years ain't pass."

My jaw clenched. "You don't know what you saw."

"I know exactly what I saw," she said. "Same CJ, same game, same spell. And you? Same weak spot."

I pressed harder on the gas. "I'm getting him out, Ti. Lawyer's lined up, paperwork ready. He deserves a shot."

"Deserves?" she repeated, voice rising. "What about what you deserve? What about not being tied to a man behind glass for the rest of your life?"

I didn't answer. Not because she was right. Not because she was wrong. Because I didn't know how to explain that "deserve" don't hit the same when history and guilt and first love get involved.

We stopped at a light and I felt her watching me. "I texted Mateo," she said finally.

I side-eyed her. "For what?"

"'Cause you ain't listening to me," she said. "So I called somebody you might." I rolled my eyes but didn't say nothing. I just drove.

Later, she told me about that visit. How she went up to Mateo's suite running her mouth, pacing his floor talking about, "She gon' mess up everything. She acting fifteen again. She wiring money, writing letters, lettin' this man still run shit from a cell."

She said Mateo just watched her, calm as always, shirt half open, cigar in hand, like the whole situation was a storm he already studied on radar. He told her, "You think Diego don't see all that?"

Tika said, "So y'all just gon' let her keep running back like it's cute?"

And Mateo, cool as ever, told her, "Sometimes you gotta let somebody walk into fire. Not to burn. To learn. When she's done, she gon' choose. And when she do? CJ not even gon' be a shadow."

When she told me that later, I acted like I didn't care. But it stuck.

A storm and a shadow. That's what they thought of me and him.

I went back to see CJ again not long after. I told myself it was about signatures and strategy, about lining up his appeal, about details Graves needed for the file.

It wasn't.

The second I sat down and picked up that phone, he smirked. "You remember that time I took you to Lenox and you almost busted your ass in them knockoff heels?" he asked.

I tried to fight my smile. "Boy, I did not almost bust my ass. The floor was slick."

"Nah," he laughed, leaning back. "You damn near face-planted in the Chick-fil-A line. I had to catch you before you wiped out in front of all them folks."

I covered my mouth, laughing in spite of myself. "You stupid."

"And you was embarrassed as hell," he went on, eyes bright. "Talkin' about, 'Everybody lookin' at me, CJ.' Ain't nobody lookin' at you but me. Always been that way."

The way he said it slid right under my defenses. No matter how much distance, no matter how much I'd grown, he still knew how to hit that soft center. "You always know how to talk shit," I said.

"Nah," he corrected, voice dropping. "I always know how to talk to you."

I went quiet. Because there was nothing I could say to that. It was true. He knew the scared girl under the mask, the angry girl hiding behind the money, the broken girl under the attitude. He'd seen every version.

"You look good," he said, softer now. "Better than I ever seen you. You got that boss glow... but I still see my girl in there."

My chest tightened. "I ain't your girl no more, CJ."

He smiled slow, that dangerous little curve. "We'll see about that."

The guard tapped the glass. Two minutes.

CJ leaned forward, pressed his lips against the glass like it was my skin. My body betrayed me, leaning up, wishing there was no barrier between us. Wishing I didn't want what I wanted.

"Don't let them play you out there," he murmured. "Ain't nobody gon' ride for you like me. Always been me and you."

When they called time and pulled us apart, I walked out with my legs low-key shaking and my heart heavier than when I came in. Again.

Now when I stepped out those gates, the sun felt disrespectful. Bright, hot, loud — like the world was celebrating something I couldn't see. My skin tingled like I'd done something I wasn't supposed to, even though all I did was sit behind glass.

Tika was waiting on the hood again, arms crossed harder this time, jaw locked. As soon as she saw the look on my face, she cussed under her breath.

"Oh my God. You cheesin' AGAIN," she said. "This man got invisible dick or somethin'?" I ignored her, walked straight to the driver side. She snatched the door before I could get in. "He talk you out your drawls through glass now?" she asked, eyes wide. "What he do, kiss the window?"

I pushed the door open anyway and slid in. I didn't answer because she was closer to the truth than I wanted to admit.

Soon as we pulled off, I grabbed my phone. My hands moved on autopilot — banking app, inmate account, CJ's name. Ten thousand. My thumb hovered for half a second.

Send.

"Uh-uh, what you doin'?" Tika snapped, trying to snatch the phone.

I yanked it back. "Chill."

"Ten racks?" she yelled. "You just sent this man ten thousand dollars? Jas, are you dumb?"

"He need it," I said, staring straight ahead.

"No the fuck he don't," she said. "He need soap, socks, and noodles. Maybe a radio. He don't need ten racks. That's a whole car note for the year. That's inventory. That's ads. That's..."

"That's my money," I snapped. "If I wanna make sure he good in there, that's what I'm gon' do."

She stared at me like she was seeing a stranger. "Fed like a king, huh?"

I looked over, eyes hard. "Watch your mouth, Ti."

"Nah, you watch yours," she shot back. "You talkin' like he sitting on some throne, not a bunk. You talkin' 'bout 'always mine' like that's romantic, not possessive. You forgetting who the fuck you are."

"And who am I?" I asked, voice low.

"You Jasmine freakin' Carter," she said, jabbing a finger at me. "You Phantum. You built a whole empire. You pullin' in more in a month than we used to see in five years. And you still lettin' a man in greens pull the strings on your heart like you a teenager."

Her words stabbed, but I couldn't even be mad. Because there was truth in them.

"You don't get it," I said quietly. "Nobody ever seen me like he does. Before the clothes. Before the photoshoots. Before the name. He knew Jasmine. The broke, scared, loud-mouthed, soft-hearted version of me. He helped build me."

"Yeah," she said, softer now. "He helped build you. Don't pretend he didn't help break you, too."

That line sat heavy between us. I didn't respond. I just drove.

Back at the condo, the city was doing what it always did — yelling, honking, flexing, hustling. But inside, it was just me, a half-melted candle, a glass of Henny, and a manila folder sitting in the center of the table like a dare.

Graves had dropped it off earlier. "Letters of support," she'd said. "Character statements. Job offers. Housing guarantees. The board needs to see he has structure waiting."

The paper looked harmless. But when I opened it and saw that blank line waiting for my words, my chest tightened up.

This wasn't just a letter. This was me putting my name, my success, my reputation on the line for the boy I loved before either one of us knew what life really was.

My phone lit up on the counter. Diego.

His name glowed bright. I watched it buzz. Watched it stop. Watched the screen go black again. I didn't pick up.

I opened my gold Cross pen and started writing.

Christopher Clark is not the man he was when he came in here. He has grown. He has learned. He has a home waiting. He has financial support. He has work opportunities. He has people who won't let him fail.

My handwriting shook, but I kept going. He is loved. Deeply. Always has been. I am prepared to take responsibility for supporting his re-entry. Not because I'm blind to his past...but because I believe in his future.

Somewhere in the middle of that paragraph, the line blurred between legal language and love letter. Tears dripped onto the page, smudging ink. I wiped my face with the back of my hand, kept writing anyway.

He deserves a second chance. A real one. And I'm willing to stand beside him when he gets it. By the time I signed my name, my chest hurt. It didn't look like some neutral statement to a board. It looked like my heart laid out in black and white.

The phone buzzed again. Diego. I turned it face down like it was too bright.

Instead, I opened my laptop, logged back into my account, and sent CJ another five racks. Just because. Just so he'd feel me. Just so when that receipt printed at commissary, he'd see my name and know he wasn't forgotten.

When the confirmation email popped up, I exhaled, long and shaky, and took the last sip of Henny like it was about to save me. Tika's words replayed in my head: He built you. He can break you, too. Then CJ's voice layered over it...always mine.

Lying in that penthouse with city lights flickering on my ceiling, the mask sitting on the table and my phone buzzing with a man who loved the woman I had become... I knew which voice still had me tied up.

I hated it. I knew it was dangerous. I knew I was playing with fire I'd already been burned by.

But in that moment? I was still his.

CHAPTER 22

Strings Attached

Atlanta nights felt heavy, pressing down on the windows like even the air was eavesdropping. Only sound was the hum of the condo's AC.

I sat on the edge of my bed, phone in my hand. For three days, I let Miami ring without an answer. But tonight? My thumb slid across the screen.

"About time," Diego's voice came through, smooth but sharp. "I was starting to think you forgot me."

I exhaled, lying back against the pillows. "I ain't forget."

"You ignoring me though."

Silence. My heart thumped.

"Jasmine," he said, and the way he used my full name made me sit up straighter. "Talk to me. You moving different. Don't think I don't notice."

I chewed my bottom lip, staring at the ceiling. "I just...I got things I need to handle. On my own."

"You ain't gotta handle shit alone," he snapped. Then softer: "That ain't how we move. If you in my circle, you in my circle. You understand?"

I hesitated, words tangling in my throat. "This is... personal. Ghosts I need to deal with. Don't worry, Diego. I got it."

His voice dropped lower, deadly calm. "Don't lie to me, Jas. I don't get lied to."

My pulse jumped. "I'm not lying. I promise. Just let me work this out, then I'll be back. For real."

He exhaled through the line, long and slow, like he was weighing whether to push harder. Finally, he said, "You better. Don't make me come to Atlanta."

Before I could respond, the floor creaked outside my door. I looked up. Tika was standing in the hall, leaning against the wall, arms folded.

"You always whisperin' in here," she said, squinting at me. "Who the hell you keep talkin' to?"

My chest tightened. "Nobody you need to worry about."

Her eyes narrowed, lips curling into a smirk that wasn't playful. "Yeah, that's what you said last time too."

I rolled over, turning my back to her and lowering my voice again. "I'll call you tomorrow, Diego," I murmured into the phone.

"Handle your ghosts," he said flatly, then hung up.

Tika was still standing there when I set the phone down. "You always got secrets," she muttered, pushing off the wall. "One day, they gon' eat you alive."

The door clicked shut, leaving me in the dark with nothing but my thoughts — and the ghosts Diego told me to handle.

I chose a spot that wasn't loud or pretty — a midtown diner with chrome sides and stubborn waitresses who didn't care who you were. I wanted a table that smelled like coffee and bacon grease, a place where hearts open easier than wallets. Tika slid into the booth first, still side-eyeing me from last night's whisper-call.

"You gon' tell me why we here?" she asked, flicking her straw paper at me.

"You'll see," I said, checking the door, palms damp even though I never sweat.

The bell chimed. She stepped in like the air belonged to her.

Keyanna.

I knew her from pictures and the tiny memories children leave behind — a laugh, a crooked braid, a face pressed to my leg at a barbecue — but time had stitched her into a woman. Almost twenty now. Memphis written in the swing of her hips, Atlanta sharpened in her gaze. She had KeKe's cheekbones and that don't-try-me mouth, but the rest? The rest looked suspiciously like me.

Honey-gold skin with a warm undertone that made cheap lighting look expensive. Hair in a high, messy puff, edges slicked, a few baby curls refusing to behave. Lashes long but not ridiculous. Nose ring, tiny hoop that caught the diner's neon. A fitted white tank - not scandalous, just confident — tucked into light-wash jeans that hugged thick thighs and a small waist. Scuffed Forces, clean laces. A jade pendant at her throat, green as a money dream.

What got me wasn't the clothes. It was the temperature around her: that low hum I learned to recognize in mirrors — pretty enough to flood a DM, dangerous enough to drain a bank.

She spotted me and grinned wide. Not shy. Not careful. Happy. It punched me right in the chest.

"Auntie Jas," she said, sliding into the booth like she'd been coming here forever. Her voice had a little rasp, like she laughed more than she cried. "You look rich."

I barked out a laugh despite myself. "You look like trouble."

"Facts," Tika muttered, eyes narrowing. "Who is this 'auntie' before I catch a charge for misidentifying minors?"

I touched Keyanna's hand. Warm. Steady. "Ti, this is Keyanna. KeKe's girl."

Tika's mouth dropped, then snapped shut so fast her lip gloss clicked. "Nuh-uh. That baby? That little baby with the barrettes that used to chew on ice? Nah. I'm old."

Keyanna smirked. "Not old, just loud." Then to me, softer, "You remember me for real? Or you just saying that?"

"I remember enough," I said, throat thickening. "And what I don't remember...I owe you."

Her eyes searched mine — the same way I've searched men, rooms, exits. She nodded like she found something she could use, then leaned back, hands folded on the table like cards.

A waitress appeared, eyed us like we might dine and dash, then softened when she recognized my face. "What y'all havin'?"

"Waffle, extra butter," I said. "Turkey bacon, hash browns scattered, onions."

"Grits," Tika added. "Heavy cheese. Coffee, black."

Keyanna tilted her head. "Blueberry pancakes. And," she glanced at me, testing, "can I get bacon and sausage?"

"Get what you want," I said. "You with me."

She smiled like she'd been told no too many times.

When the waitress left, silence settled — not awkward, just new. I watched how Keyanna's fingers drummed the table, a rhythm I recognized from a thousand nervous hustles. I watched how her eyes cut to the door, to the register, to the street. Alert. Counting. Measuring.

"Where you staying?" I asked.

"A friend's spot," she said, shrugging. "It's cool. Couch comfy. Don't worry."

"I didn't ask if it was comfy," I said. "I asked where."

She smirked. "You gon' pop up with a flashlight and a robe like a probation officer?"

"Don't test me," I said, smiling. "I'll show up with a mortgage."

Tika whistled. "She serious, baby. She buys neighborhoods when she bored."

Keyanna's eyes flicked to me again, softer now. "You always like this?"

"Like what?"

"Rescue and run," she said lightly. "Look like a storm but move like a blueprint." That line slid right under my ribs. I could feel Tika looking at me but I didn't turn.

"I ain't come to rescue," I said. "I came to claim."

"Claim what?"

"Family."

She went still. The diner noise faded for a breath.

Our food landed, plates clattering, syrup sweating. We ate a few bites in a comfortable silence. I let her drown pancakes in syrup. I let her talk first.

"You left," she said finally, not angry. Just true. "Not just Atlanta. You left us. I don't need the story today. But I need to know if you plan on leaving again."

Tika coughed like the truth had bones. I put my fork down. "I'm not gonna lie to you. I leave often. I move. I disappear. That's how I lived long enough to get here. But you? I won't leave you again. Not without a map to where I'm going and a key to the door."

She held my stare for a long time. Then nodded once. "Aight."

The tension broke. She started talking like a dam had cracked—little pieces of life tossed across the table: side jobs, a hairstylist aunt on the other side of town who charged family full price, a manager at a strip-mall boutique trying to "mentor" her into unpaid hours, a dude with a fast car and slower hands she already blocked.

Community college plans that felt like "standing still," a TikTok she refused to dance on, a stack of notebooks in her bag full of ideas for a small brand she didn't know how to start: Key Cut — custom cropped tops, reworked jackets, bold stitching.

"Let me see," I said.

She hesitated — then slid one of the notebooks over. Graph paper, pencil lines, little notes in the margins. She'd measured seams. She'd budgeted threads. I read silent while she pretended not to watch me read.

"These are good," I said. Her sketches were clean. Her ideas were real.

"Everybody say that," she muttered, embarrassed by the compliment she wanted.

"I don't," I said. "I say what pays."

Her lips twitched. "So pay me then."

Tika snorted. "Oh, she definitely your kin."

I leaned back. "What do you need?"

"Space," she said, surprising me with the speed of the answer. "Not a bedroom. A workspace. A heavy machine that don't jam, not that Walmart joint. Good shears. A dress form. Light. And time I don't gotta trade for fourteen dollars an hour."

I did the math without showing it. A studio could be lined up in a day. Machines, tools, an assistant to deal with errands. A small grant through a shell so her name wasn't screaming mine.

"You'll have it," I said.

She blinked, mask slipping. "For real?"

"For real," I said. "With conditions."

She rolled her eyes, but her smile gave her away. "Knew it."

"Condition one: school's optional if you got output. You don't owe a degree to nobody. But you owe progress to yourself. I wanna see samples on a schedule. Deadlines. Two pieces a week, minimum. Miss twice, studio locks until you catch up." She nodded, already calculating.

"Condition two: no boyfriends in the workspace. Not even the ones that bring food."

"Clearly you projecting," Tika said, deadpan.

I ignored her. "Condition three: cash discipline. I'll set a budget. You'll spend it. You'll track it. I'll audit it. There will be quizzes."

Keyanna's laugh cracked open her face. "Who are you, IRS Barbie?"

"Condition four," I said, leaning in, tone dropping, "you don't go where I go. Not yet. My lanes cut deep. I don't want your tires on them. You build clean while I wash dirty."

The humor left her eyes. Pride tried to rise; humility shoved it down. "So I'm on the bench."

"You the franchise," I said. "The bench is where we protect value."

She stared another second, then nodded. "Okay."

Tika cleared her throat. "Say thank you, child."

Keyanna's gaze softened. She reached across the table and squeezed my fingers. "Thank you."

It landed warm and heavy. I squeezed back.

The bell over the door chimed again — a dude in a hoodie stepped in, looked around like he was shopping for wallets, then thought better and left. I clocked him; so did Keyanna. Her eyes followed clean. Good instincts. I filed that away.

"What you doing after this?" I asked.

She shrugged. "Catching the bus. That couch won't warm itself."

"Cancel that," I said. "You're coming with us."

"To your place?" she asked, cautious but hopeful.

"Temporarily," I said. "You'll have a room. We'll get you a studio by next week. You'll sign paperwork. It'll be real. But listen to me: when I give you keys, you don't lose them. When I give you budget, you don't burn it on vibes. When I put my name behind yours, you don't let nobody touch it with sticky hands. Copy?"

She swallowed, then straightened. "Copy."

Tika grinned. "Ooh, I can't wait to boss you around about thread counts."

"Please don't," Keyanna deadpanned. "You look like you call glitter 'sparkles' and try to glue it to denim."

I slapped the table, cackling. The waitress jumped. "She yours," Tika said, shaking her head. "Lord help us."

We paid. Outside, the sky sat low and bruised. Atlanta looked like it wanted to storm but hadn't made up its mind. We walked to the car, the street humming with little dangers. A group of boys posted by the corner store went quiet as we passed — respect or threat, hard to tell. One tried a whistle. Keyanna didn't flinch, didn't speed up. She just looked once, let him see the math on her face, and kept going.

"That part," Tika said under her breath.

At the curb, I touched Keyanna's shoulder. "One more condition."

She arched a brow. "Damn, how many levels this game got?"

"Enough," I said. "When you feel the itch to prove you're grown by doing something stupid, call me before you do it. Not after."

She bit her lip, thinking, then nodded. "You answer?"

"I will," I said, meaning it more than I liked.

We slid into the SUV. As I pulled off, Keyanna sank into the seat and whispered, almost to herself, "This the first time in a while I felt...pointed."

"Pointed?" Tika asked.

"Like a compass," she said. "Not just spinning."

I kept my eyes on the road. "Good. Keep it pointed."

My phone vibrated in the console. A Miami number. I didn't look. Not with Keyanna in the backseat and Tika pretending not to clock my nerves.

For a few blocks, I let myself breathe. Family beside me. Future behind me. Trouble calling on mute.

At a red light, Keyanna leaned forward between us. "Auntie?"

"Yeah, baby."

"Do I gotta call you 'Auntie' in public?"

"What you wanna call me?"

She grinned. "Boss."

Tika groaned. "Lord."

I smiled despite everything. "Earn it."

"I will," she said, like a promise to God.

The light turned green. We drove.

The condo felt different with Keyanna walking through it. Usually the place smelled like candles and money — faint traces of Dior perfume, leather from the couch, a whisper of champagne corks still in the trash. But tonight, with her bags in the foyer and her sneakers squeaking against marble, it felt like something else. Family. Something I wasn't sure I deserved anymore.

Keyanna stopped in the middle of the living room, spinning slow like she was standing inside a dream. "Damn," she whispered. "This how you livin'?"

I leaned against the kitchen counter, arms folded. "This is how you could be livin'... if you keep your shit tight."

She smirked. "Sounds like the start of a lecture."

"It is." I nodded toward the hall. "You got the guest room at the end. Closet space, queen bed, TV mounted. Bathroom's yours. But there's rules."

"Of course there's rules," she said, plopping on the couch like she already paid rent. "Lay 'em out."

I counted them on my fingers. "One: no boys up in here. None. I don't care if it's a cousin, classmate, your so-called bestie with a penis. This ain't the trap, and it damn sure ain't no love motel."

She groaned. "Auntie—"

I cut her off sharp. "No boys." She rolled her eyes but nodded.

"Two: no street hangouts. If you got friends, they meet you at the diner, the studio, or the mall. I catch you posted on some corner makin' noise? You're out. No questions asked."

"Damn," she muttered. "You runnin' this like probation."

"Three," I continued, ignoring the jab, "you tell me where you go. I don't need play-by-plays, but I need location. If shit go down, I need to know where to pull up."

Her smirk faded. She sat up straighter. "So basically, you tryna keep me from ending up like my mama."

The words punched me in the gut. I stayed quiet, jaw locked.

Keyanna tilted her head, watching me carefully. "I don't remember much about her. Bits and pieces, ya know? But what I do know? She ain't deserve what happened. People always whisper it was some street shit. That's why I never met my pops. He dipped. Never showed his face. Probably the same motherfucker that got her killed."

Her voice cracked, but her eyes didn't. They burned steady, like coals that had been waiting on fuel.

"One day," she said, softer now, "I'm gonna find out who he is. And when I do? I'm gonna make him pay."

I froze, staring at her.

All those nights in the projects, whispers floating around about KeKe's death. Rumors about who set her up, who pulled the strings, who left her bleeding while Keyanna cried in a crib.

But I couldn't say it. Not tonight. Not when she was sitting here looking at me like I was the only family she had left.

So I swallowed the truth, forced my voice steady. "You ain't gotta worry about that right now. What you need to focus on is building your lane, not chasing ghosts. Let me handle the streets. You handle the future."

Keyanna leaned back, arms crossed, eyes still hot. "Future ain't shit without justice."

Her words hung in the air heavy, heavier than the designer chandelier swaying above us.

Tika shifted on the loveseat, uncomfortable. "Jas," she said softly, "maybe this ain't—"

"I said I'll handle it," I snapped sharper than I meant.

The silence after was brutal.

Finally, Keyanna nodded slow, not happy but not fighting. "Fine. I'll follow the rules. No boys, no corners, no lies. But don't think I'm lettin' this go. One way or another, I'm gettin' answers."

She stood, grabbed her bag, and disappeared down the hall. The door clicked shut behind her.

Tika gave me a look that said everything. This is a storm. And you just brought it inside your house.

I poured myself a drink, staring at the closed door. The taste of liquor burned, but not as much as the truth I kept locked behind my teeth.

The condo had gone quiet for the night. Tika crashed on the couch, Keyanna's door stayed shut, and Atlanta outside was doing what it always did — buzzing, flexing, breaking, living.

I stretched out on my bed, silk sheets soft against my skin, phone glowing in my hand. Two names kept lighting the screen like dueling neon signs.

Diego: steady. Short messages, always sharp, always firm. Where you at? ... You good? ... Don't forget who you are.

CJ: wild. Calls late as hell through static-filled prison lines. His voice always pulling me back.

I laid there staring at the screen, thumb hovering over both. Finally, I hit CJ.

"Baby," he said, that smooth poison dripping through the line, "I thought you forgot me again."

I smiled despite myself, rolling onto my side. "I been busy."

"Busy doin' what? Playin' rich girl? Shopping sprees and champagne? You know that ain't really you. You mine, Jas. Always been. Always gon' be."

I bit my lip, silence heavy between us.

"You write that letter?" he asked.

"Yeah."

"You make me sound good?"

I smirked. "I made you sound like a damn angel. If they don't let you out, it's 'cause God ain't ready."

He laughed loud, deep, the kind of laugh that made my chest ache with nostalgia. "That's why I love you."

On the nightstand, my phone buzzed again. Diego.

I flipped it face down.

"You still there?" CJ asked in my ear.

"Yeah, I'm here."

For a while, we just breathed together, his voice painting old memories, mine carrying him promises I wasn't sure I could keep.

The door creaked open. I glanced up.

Tika stood in the hall, hair messy from sleep, eyes squinting at me. She leaned on the doorframe, arms folded.

"You always smiling when you on that phone," she muttered. "Who the hell got you cheesin' like that?"

I covered the receiver. "Mind your business, Ti."

She shook her head, lips curling into that smirk that meant trouble. "Mm-hmm. Secrets gon' kill you faster than bullets."

She shut the door slow, leaving me in the glow of CJ's voice.

"Who you talkin' to?" he asked, sharp now.

"Nobody," I said quick. "Just Ti being nosy."

"Keep her out your shit," he said. "This between me and you."

I swallowed, nodded even though he couldn't see me. "Yeah. Just me and you." But when the line went dead, I rolled over and stared at the other phone lighting up. Diego. Message after message stacking up.

I didn't answer. I couldn't. Because in that moment, tangled in two worlds, I wanted both.

The condo was too full and too quiet at the same time. I padded barefoot through the halls, glass of wine in one hand, phone in the other, and everywhere I turned there was something pressing on me.

Keyanna's door was shut, light still glowing underneath. The girl had energy like a live wire — I could hear faint music bleeding through, some Memphis trap on low, her pen scratching quick in that sketchbook. She had her mama's fight and my face. Dangerous combination.

Tika was stretched out on the couch, fake-sleeping, blanket only half over her body. I knew she wasn't out cold. She breathed too sharp, like she was waiting for me to slip. Always watching me these days.

And then there was me — walking around my own damn condo like a stranger, restless, caught between past and future, ghosts and promises.

I sat on the balcony, city lights blinking like they knew my secrets. Atlanta was loud tonight — bikes revving down Peachtree, sirens chasing shadows, bass rattling from somebody's rooftop party. But up here? It was just me and the wine.

I pulled up a picture on my phone — not of money, not of cars, not even of CJ. It was a picture I'd snapped earlier at the diner. Keyanna, mid-laugh, syrup on her chin, flipping me off when I teased her about eating like a linebacker. The smile damn near cracked the screen.

I whispered to myself, low: "I got you, baby girl. You don't even know yet."

I meant it.

But the phone buzzed before the promise could settle.

CJ CALLING

I stared at the screen so long my wine got warm. His name glowed like temptation itself. I could already hear his voice, already feel the pull wrapping me up like vines.

My thumb hovered. Then — buzz. Another name lit the screen.

Diego.

Two men, two worlds, two different futures — both pulling me like I was a rope they wanted to tug 'til I snapped. I set the wine down, heart slamming.

CJ's call cut off. Diego's buzzed again.

And then I heard it — a soft shuffle at the balcony door. Tika. Hair wild, blanket dragged around her shoulders like a cape.

"You ain't slick," she said, voice low, eyes sharp. "You out here juggling calls like a teenager."

I forced a laugh. "Go back to sleep, Ti."

She stepped closer, leaning on the doorframe. "I ain't sleep. I heard you whisperin' earlier. Smilin' like he hung the damn moon. And now you sittin' here starin' at your phone like it's a slot machine."

I turned the phone face down. "It ain't what you think."

"It's always exactly what I think with you," she shot back. "You think I don't know you by now? One's that jailbird got your heart in a chokehold, the other's that billionaire with patience I don't even understand. And you out here tryin' to eat your cake and your ice cream too."

Her words burned 'cause they were true.

"I can handle it," I said, more to myself than her.

She laughed sharp. "Handle it? Jas, you got your niece under your roof now. A girl who

252

don't even know half the shit that went down with her mama. She look at you like God, and you out here playin' tug-of-war with ghosts. That ain't handlin' shit. That's crashin' in slow motion."

I didn't answer. Couldn't.

Instead, I picked up the phone again, thumb brushing the screen like it was skin.

"Whoever you pick," Tika said softer now, "just don't let it kill you. Or her." She jerked her chin toward Keyanna's door.

Then she left me on the balcony with the weight of it all.

The phone buzzed again. CJ CALLING. And this time? I answered.

CHAPTER

23

Ghost Ties

The law office smelled like polish and paper. Too clean, too cold — the kind of place where lives get signed away or rewritten depending on what name sits on the letterhead.

I sat there in my skin-tight black jumpsuit, Chanel bag on the table like a statement, nails tapping against the wood. My foot wouldn't stop bouncing. I hated waiting, but this wasn't just waiting. This was the moment.

The receptionist gave me that polite smile she gave everyone — eyes dipping just a little too long at the Rolex on my wrist before she looked away. She knew money when she saw it. But what she didn't know was how bad my chest was thumping under all this gloss.

CJ.

Every second dragged me back to him — the glass, the phone, the smell of prison air on his clothes when I leaned too close on visitation days. And now? All this time, all these wires to his books, all these letters I wrote like love songs to a parole board that didn't give a damn...it was coming down to this office, this man behind a mahogany desk with too-white teeth.

The door opened with a soft click.

"Ms. Jasmine?"

I stood up before he finished, legs shaky under the heels I wore like armor. "Yes."

"Come on back," he said, holding the door open with a practiced sweep. His suit was tailored but not flashy, navy blue, tie knotted tight. His office was bigger than my first apartment — shelves lined with leather-bound books, framed degrees, a city view stretching behind glass. Graves said he would be worth the extra money; at least he spends it well.

I sat, crossing my legs slow, pretending my heart wasn't punching my ribs.

He adjusted his glasses, flipped open a folder. "We've been waiting on the parole board's final decision for a while now, but I've got good news for you today."

My breath caught. "Good news?"

His lips curved into a calm smile. "Christopher Clark Jr. has been granted parole. He'll be released within the next thirty days."

I swear the room spun. My hand flew to my chest like I could hold my heart in place.

"You serious?" My voice cracked, too sharp.

"Completely." He pushed the paperwork toward me, tapping a line of typed words that might as well have been neon. "Parole granted. Pending final administrative release. He'll have to meet certain conditions, of course — employment plan, residence confirmation, regular check-ins — but yes, Ms. Jasmine. He's coming home."

For a second, I couldn't breathe. Couldn't move. Just sat there staring at the words that changed everything.

CJ. Coming home.

I laughed — sharp, disbelieving — then covered my mouth. My eyes burned hot, mascara threatening to slide. I leaned back, trying to play it cool, but my whole body was trembling.

"I... I didn't think..."

The lawyer's voice softened. "Very few men make it out on their first hearing. His record inside was clean. No infractions in years. Plus your letters carried weight." He gave me a look. "The board likes to see strong support networks. Family. Stability. And, frankly, your presence here matters."

My throat was dry as sand. "He's really getting out?"

"Yes," he said firmly. "Within thirty days. Congratulations, Ms. Clark." as if I was his wife.

I almost wanted to hug him, but instead I leaned forward, elbows on the desk, nails digging into my palms. A rush hit me so hard it felt like standing too fast.

CJ's voice in my head: Always mine.

I swallowed hard, tried to gather myself. "Okay. So... what do I need to do?"

"We'll need to finalize his residential plan. Where will he be staying? Does he have employment lined up? These are the questions the parole officer will ask right away."

"I got him," I said instantly. Too fast. Too hard. "He got a place. With me. He ain't gonna need for nothing."

The lawyer studied me, pen tapping. "That's good. The stronger the structure, the better. You're certain you're ready for that responsibility?"

I lifted my chin, heat rising in my chest. "He been locked away twenty years. I been ready."

And it was true. Through all the hustles, the gloss, the Rolls Royces and diamonds, through Miami trips and Dubai licks, through Diego's steady love and Tika's nagging warnings — I never shook CJ. He built me. I owed him.

And now? He was coming home.

The elevator doors slid shut and I finally let the scream out — quiet, trapped in my throat, shoulders shaking like a laugh that forgot it was a laugh. I pressed my palms flat against the cool brass rails and breathed until the numbers stopped blurring.

The lobby smelled like citrus cleaner and ambition. People in suits crossed marble like chess pieces, but none of them felt real anymore. Outside, Peachtree was a river — horns, buses, sunlight knifing down between buildings. The heat slapped me in the face and felt like blessing.

I put on my shades. Then I pulled out my phone.

TIKA.

She answered on the second ring. "You good? You sound like you ran a marathon."

"CJ made parole," I said. It came out like a secret and a victory at once. "They granting it. Thirty days. Maybe sooner."

Silence. Then a sharp inhale, a muttered curse. "You serious?"

"Dead ass."

"Damn." Another breath. Her voice softened, complicated. "Okay. Okay... okay. So what we doing?"

"We getting ready," I said, already walking fast toward the garage. "He needs a place, clothes, a phone, lawyer follow-ups, PO schedule — all of it clean, all of it tight. I want day one perfect."

Tika whistled. "You shining like a Christmas tree right now, ain't you?"

I smiled despite myself. "Shut up. Bring the truck. Meet me at Lenox. We starting with clothes."

"Say less."

I hung up before my brain could spin into the places it liked to hide. The call screen faded and another name sat there like a dare. CJ.

My thumb hovered.

Not yet. I wanted to hear his voice with a plan in my hand, not just joy in my mouth. He'd smell the difference. He always did.

The Range pulled out into traffic like it was parting water. I rolled the window down and let the city blow hot across my face. For once Atlanta didn't feel like a weight; it felt like a runway.

At Lenox, the air-conditioning hit and the scent changed to leather and new money. Security nodded like they remembered me. Maybe they did. I'd come here angry and lonely and godlike for years. Today I was something else. Expectant.

Tika found me near men's tailoring, hair wrapped in a scarf, sliding her shades up. "Look at you," she said, reading my face. "Whole aura different."

"Don't start," I warned, but the grin betrayed me.

We moved like a mission. White button-downs that actually fit his shoulders. A navy suit — not flashy, just grown. Crisp T-shirts, dark denim. Joggers for quiet mornings. A pair of clean Forces because some rituals matter. I ran a hand across ties and skipped them; CJ always hated leashes.

"What size is he now?" the associate asked, tape around his neck.

"Well, I knew then," I hesitated, "but he been lifting."

"We'll tailor to both," he said, already pinning options for alterations.

I added socks, boxers, undershirts — things nobody cheers for but freedom feels like them when you pull them on without asking. A leather wallet I knew he'd pretend was "too much" and keep anyway. A cologne that was wood and skin and not too loud. He'd been trapped in disinfectant and concrete for two decades — outside should smell like choices.

At checkout, Tika leaned on the counter and studied me. "How you feeling? For real."

I exhaled. "Like I been holding my breath twenty years."

"And Diego?" She said it light, like tasting the name.

"Diego knows I got ghosts."

"Ghosts don't usually ask for drawers and a PO schedule," she muttered.

I didn't take the bait. We loaded the bags into the truck. Sun flashed off chrome. I checked my phone again. Still didn't call. Instead I texted Attorney Graves: Got the news. Send full conditions list + tentative release date once stamped. I'll handle residence +

employment plan. She replied in under a minute: On it.

Employment. He wasn't clocking in anywhere. But the board needed lines and signatures.

I drove us to a small property I kept quiet — not my penthouse, not the flashy midtown unit. A tidy brownstone on a quiet street with oak trees leaning over it like old ladies in church. Brick steps. Black door. Privacy. The kind of place you could exhale without the city climbing through the window.

"You moving him here?" Tika asked, stepping into the cool foyer.

"For the first months," I said. "No distractions. He learns the rhythm out here, not back in chaos."

We walked the space. Sun through white curtains. A couch that invited sleep. Kitchen that said home without shouting it. I opened a hall closet and checked the safe, changed the code.

Upstairs, I opened the primary closet and pushed my unused coats back. Empty hangers stared at me like open hands. I hung the suit bag, lined the shelves with folded tees. Tika shook out the Forces and set them straight by the door like a welcome mat.

You really doing this," she said softly. Not judgment.

"Yeah."

We made lists out loud as we moved. "Barber," Tika said. "He ain't walking out with them state edges."

"Doctor," I said. "Full workup. He ain't touched real care in decades."

"Phone."

"Bank account."

"PO schedule."

"Gym membership."

"Clippers. He gonna say he don't need 'em and then keep 'em by the sink."

We laughed, and the sound felt good, like everything in my body loosened a notch. In the bedroom, I sat on the edge of the bed and let the quiet stretch.

"What about Keyanna?" Tika asked, gentle this time. "You bringing him by the condo? Or...?"

"Not yet," I said. "He needs to learn my rules before he meets my world."

"And Diego?" She said it because she loves me and because she hates when I float.

My phone buzzed — Graves again: Preliminary release window: 18–28 days. Conditions attached. A PDF slid in behind it. I opened it — residency confirmed; employment required within 30 days; weekly check-ins; curfew; no contact with felons. My eyes snagged on the last one and kept going.

"We good?" Tika asked.

"We good," I said. "We better than good."

Outside, wind pushed through the oaks and made the leaves whisper. The house felt alive, like it was already learning his weight. I stood in the doorway and imagined keys turning. A bag dropping. A man who'd been broken by time stepping into a space I built with the same hands that once hid guns in shoeboxes.

On the drive back, the city looked brighter and meaner at once. Atlanta smiled for you even when it was sharpening knives. I answered three calls — a rental company about staging the warehouse "birthday party," a security guy I trusted from a past life, a chef who understood discretion. I spoke in code because I hadn't unlearned that language.

"Date flexible?" the rental woman asked.

"Soon," I said. "I'll pay for the hold."

"Theme?"

"Homecoming," I said, smiling.

In the mirror, Tika studied me. "You throwing this for him... or for you?"

"Both," I said. "He needs to walk into light."

"And the warehouse?"

I kept my eyes on the road. "Insurance. Private. No cameras. No surprises."

She didn't push. She didn't have to. We both knew what private meant in my mouth.

My phone buzzed again while we passed the Varsity. I didn't have to look to know the name. CJ. This time I answered.

Static, a click, then his voice. "Say it again."

I laughed. "You don't even know what I'm about to say."

"I know," he said, that warmth sliding right into my bones. "I could hear it in your breath."

"You free," I whispered. "Parole granted. Thirty days or less."

Silence. Then a sound I hadn't heard from him since the first summer — joy stripped bare. "Damn, baby. Damn."

I pulled the truck to the curb and let my forehead rest on the wheel, eyes stinging. Tika stared out the window to give me the illusion of privacy.

"I got you," I said. "I got a place. Clothes. Everything. You don't gotta touch dirt when you step out."

He went quiet again, then: "I knew you was gon' do it. I knew you would." His voice roughened. "That's why you mine. You always been mine."

The words hit different now — not a chain, more like a brand I'd chosen. I closed my eyes and let them warm me.

"When I come home," he said, voice dropping, "it's me and you. No more glass. No more phones. I'm touching the world with both hands. I'm touching you."

I felt Tika's energy spike beside me and turned the volume down a notch. "One step at a time," I said, smiling. "Paper first. Then the rest."

"You sound like a boss."

"I am."

He laughed, proud. "Aight, Boss. Put me down for whatever you need."

"Whatever you need," I corrected. "I'm handling it. And CJ?"

"Yeah?"

"No mistakes. Not one. You hear me?"

He didn't hesitate. "I hear you. Loud."

We hung up. I sat there a moment and let the city fill the quiet. Tika finally spoke.

"You sure?" she asked softly.

"No," I said. "I'm certain."

She made a face. "Same thing."

We drove home and the day started moving faster, like time finally believed me. Deliveries got scheduled. The brownstone got cleaned. A barber confirmed a home visit for "a private client." I forwarded Graves the address and confirmed I'd act as point-of-contact for the PO.

Back at the condo, Keyanna's door opened to the smell of hot glue and fabric. She held up a half-finished crop jacket with strong shoulders and wild hand-stitched edges. "First sample," she said, chin tipped up.

"It's fire," I said, meaning it.

"I know," she grinned. "Can I model it?"

"Tomorrow," with my most reassuring nod. "Tonight we planning."

"For what?"

"Family business," Tika said, breezing past with her laptop. "This is going to be a night to remember...and I'm really not invited to this extravaganza?" She was clearly hurt and confused.

I didn't know if she would spoil the night and I wanted it to go a certain way. "Not this time Tika. I got you on the next one baby girl. Let me handle the welcome home".

I stared at the text from Diego, rubbing sleep from my eyes. My silk scarf had slipped, hair puffed around my face. The city outside was still gray, streetlights buzzing tired.

Atlanta. I need you here, I typed back. Then, after a pause: Today.

Three dots. Then his reply: Flight wheels down at noon.

My chest tightened. Diego never hesitated. When I asked, he moved. That loyalty scared me more than CJ's absence sometimes. Because with Diego, there weren't chains, just choice — and choice can cut deeper than steel.

By the time he landed, I had my armor on: olive jumpsuit belted tight, shades, lips glossy. Tika rode shotgun, Keyanna in the back with her notebook, eyes wide at the private terminal like she'd never seen jets that close. She hadn't.

Diego stepped off his plane in a cream suit, no tie, watch gleaming under the noon sun. He kissed my cheek like always, slow and deliberate, hands lingering a second longer than friendly. His cologne wrapped around me — cedar, citrus, control.

"You asked," he said, voice low. "I came."

I nodded. "Let's see the spots."

The first spot sat off Auburn, a hulking brick building with steel doors and faded graffiti tagged across the side. Inside, dust motes floated in wide beams of light cutting through high windows. The space was cavernous, echoes bouncing off exposed beams.

"Plenty of room for whatever story you tell," Diego said, walking slow, hands behind his back like a general inspecting troops. "Private lot out back, loading dock. Easy to control access. Cameras easy to install...or remove."

Tika looked around, unimpressed. "Feels loud. Too many eyes on Auburn these days. Gentrifiers walking they dogs and calling 12 if a leaf moves wrong."

Diego smirked. "She's not wrong."

I walked the length of the space, heels clicking on the concrete. I could see it already: a party that looked like love, smelled like freedom, tasted like celebration. Champagne towers in the front, shadows in the back. Two different truths in one room.

"It'll work," I said.

Diego tilted his head. "You're sure?"

I looked him dead in the eye. "I know how to build a stage. And I know how to end a play. Cancel the other showings."

He studied me for a beat, then nodded. "Then Auburn it is."

We walked back out into the heat. Keyanna trailed, snapping photos on her phone, eyes bright like she was cataloguing a world she wanted in on.

Tika leaned close, muttering, "You better tell him the whole story sooner or later."

"Not today," I said.

When Keyanna hopped in the car ahead of us, Diego caught my wrist, turning me toward him. His eyes were sharp but his touch was steady.

"You asked me to come here to Atlanta. That wasn't the only reason was it? I can feel it — you need more than my opinion on a warehouse."

I swallowed. "I need a promise."

He raised a brow. "A promise?"

"That no matter what ghosts walk in that room, no matter what I've done or where I came from...you'll still see me the way you do now. Not broken. Not dirty. Just me."

For a moment, his jaw worked, silent. Then he stepped closer, voice low so only I could hear.

"Jas, I don't love pieces of people. I love storms. You're a storm. And storms don't scare me. They feed me."

My throat tightened.

"You want a promise?" he said, brushing his thumb across my knuckles. "Here's mine. There's nothing in your past that can undo what I feel for you right now. Nothing."

It shook me more than I wanted to admit.

I pulled my hand back, smirking to cover the quake. "Careful. I might hold you to that."

"Do," he said simply.

Back at the condo that night, I spread papers across the glass dining table like a war map. Parole conditions. Release window. Vendor contacts. Employment drafts.

Tika poured wine and leaned against the counter. "You treating this like a wedding."

"It is," I muttered, scribbling. "A wedding to freedom." I wrote in neat lines:

Day One:

Pickup (private car, tinted).

Outfit staged.

Barber on call.

Brownstone ready.

Phones (burner + iPhone).

Meal: steak, lobster, cheesecake.

Day Seven:

Bank account funded.

Employment letter filed.

Warehouse "party."

PO check confirmed.

No loose ends.

I circled the last line hard. No loose ends.

Tika read over my shoulder and shook her head. "Girl, you planning a victory lap and a funeral at the same time."

"Maybe," I said, sipping wine. "But one thing's for sure...when CJ steps out, he's stepping into my world. Not back into the one that almost killed him."

My place was quiet except for the scratch of my pen on paper. Midnight spread across Atlanta, the skyline glowing like a crown outside the windows. My wine was gone, cold glass sweating rings into the table, but my mind was sharper than ever.

I went over the checklist again, lips moving soundless. "Car. Clothes. Brownstone. Party. No loose ends."

The words kept circling until they were a chant.

I didn't hear her at first.

"Auntie?"

I jumped, pen clattering against the table.

Keyanna stood in the hallway, oversized T-shirt swallowing her frame, curls tied up in a scarf. Her eyes were curious, bright even at this hour. She glanced at the papers scattered like puzzle pieces.

"Who's CJ?"

The name on her lips made my chest seize.

She'd heard me — I must've said it out loud, maybe whispering like a prayer.

I forced a calm smile, sliding my hand across the papers like they were nothing. "You should be asleep, baby girl."

She tilted her head, unconvinced. "I asked a question."

Her tone wasn't disrespectful. Just sharp. Straight to the point. KeeKee's tone. "CJ," she repeated. "Who is he? Some business partner? One of them dudes you always hiding from us?"

I opened my mouth, but the words wouldn't come. My tongue felt heavy, throat dry. Finally, I stood, walked to her, and touched her cheek. "Don't worry about CJ. Not tonight."

Her eyes narrowed, searching me. "That mean yes or no?"

"That mean," I said softly, "I got things I carry so you don't have to. And this is one of 'em."

She flinched, hurt flickering across her face, but she covered it quick, shrugging like it didn't matter. "Fine. Keep your secrets. Just don't let 'em burn the house down."

She turned and padded back to her room, door shutting with a soft click that felt louder than a gunshot.

I stood there frozen, papers under my palm, heart heavy.

Because I knew one day I'd have to answer. And when that day came, everything — CJ, Diego, Keyanna, even me — would snap like brittle glass.

But not tonight. Tonight I had work.

I sat back down, pen shaking in my fingers, and wrote his name again at the top of the page: CJ – Day One.

The letters stared back at me like a dare.

The quiet settled in again, but Keyanna's question still hung in the air like smoke.

Who's CJ?

I couldn't shake it. Couldn't scrub it from my skin.

So I stepped out onto the balcony. Atlanta lay stretched beneath me, glittering and humming, the freeway snaking like a lit fuse through the dark. A storm was brewing somewhere south; I could smell the wet concrete waiting.

I gripped the railing, let the city air slap against my face, hot and dirty but alive.

"He's coming home," I whispered.

The words slid out raw, for me and nobody else.

"CJ's coming home."

My chest ached saying it. Half joy, half fear.

I closed my eyes and pictured it — him stepping out in the clothes I bought, the leather of the new Forces creasing under his first free steps, his laugh cutting through all the years that stole it from me. His arms around me, warm, real.

I wanted that so bad it scared me.

And yet, underneath, a voice hissed: Ghosts don't die when you set them free. They come back louder.

I ignored it. I pressed my forehead against the railing and breathed deep, like maybe the city could carry the secret for me.

"You're mine," I murmured to the night, to him, to myself. "Always been mine. Always will be."

The words sank into the skyline, swallowed by engines and sirens, and for a moment I believed them.

Then my phone buzzed again. His name lighting up the screen.

CJ CALLING.

I didn't answer. Not this time. I slid the phone face-down and let the city hold me until the storm finally broke.

Rain started to fall, hard and sudden, washing the glass, soaking the balcony. It felt like baptism. It felt like warning.

Either way, tomorrow was coming fast.

Tika eased in and dropped a bag from the fish spot out in the West End on the counter. Keyanna was sprawled on the couch, sketchbook open, pretending not to listen; Tika pulled me in close and whispered too loud. "You hear what folks saying?" she asked, peeling styrofoam open, steam rolling out.

"Donna name all in mouths again. Streets buzzing."

I leaned in. "What they saying?"

"That she vanished. Ain't been seen in weeks...heard one laugh that 'nobody vanish in Atlanta. They get tucked.' I heard it myself, and if people floatin' shit like that waiting for their french fries, you know they talkin' in barber shops and beauty parlors."

I sipped my wine, voice flat. "Let 'em buzz. Bees die after they sting."

She narrowed her eyes, not finding it funny at all. "Bees leave bodies too, Jas. You ready for that?" Her look said more. Like I been scribbling plans and pretending the world gonna play along. She's worried the ghosts start pulling receipts.

Then she pointed her head toward Keyanna, who was pretending harder now, pencil scratching. "That girl smarter than she let on."

"Yeah," I muttered. "That's what I'm afraid of." The room went quiet, except for the rain still sliding down the windows.

Sometimes you gotta act like life regular, even when it's not. That's why I told Tika, "Forget fried fish in a box. Get dressed. We taking Keyanna out. No business. No plotting. Just dinner."

She gave me a look like she ain't believe me, but she went along anyway.

We hit one of those midtown spots with low lights and leather booths, the kind where you don't gotta yell over the music but you still feel the bass under your feet. Waiters moved smooth, wine glasses clinked, laughter spilled from tables.

For a second, I could almost pretend we was just three women — auntie, niece, cousin — eating a meal.

Keyanna looked grown under that glow. She'd thrown on a little black dress that hugged her hips just enough to show she wasn't no kid anymore, curls wild around her face. Her nails tapped against the menu, eyes darting like she was studying the room as much as the food.

"Get whatever you want," I told her, sliding the menu back.

She smirked. "Say less."

Tika laughed, already ordering a cocktail. "Girl gon' run the bill up first chance she get."

"I learned from the best," Keyanna shot back, looking at me with a grin.

I smiled, but inside my chest tightened. She was sharp. Too sharp.

Dinner started easy. Steak, pasta, glasses of wine (for me and Tika), Shirley Temple for

Keyanna. We joked, laughed, shaded the people walking by. Normal.

But then Keyanna leaned in, her voice quieter. "So...can I ask y'all something?"

I froze with my fork halfway to my mouth. Tika caught it too, her smile dropping a notch.

"What's up, baby girl?" I asked, careful.

Keyanna's eyes flicked between us. "My mama. KeeKee. Y'all don't never talk about her. Not really. And I been wondering... who was my daddy?"

The question dropped like a gunshot. The music didn't cover it. The clinking glasses didn't cover it.

I felt heat crawl up my neck. Tika set her drink down too hard, eyes on me like don't you dare say nothing.

Keyanna kept going. "I mean, I know she was wild. I know she got caught up. But...I deserve to know, right? I deserve to know who he was. Why he never came around. Why he let her—" She stopped, eyes shining. "Why he let her die."

I couldn't breathe for a second. My hand gripped the napkin in my lap until it twisted tight.

"Keyanna," I said softly. "Some answers don't heal you. They cut you deeper."

She frowned. "That ain't fair."

"No, it ain't," I admitted. My throat burned. "But life ain't fair. All I can tell you is your mama loved you. She wasn't perfect, but she loved you."

"That ain't what I asked," she shot back.

The table went silent. Tika sipped her drink slow, like she wanted to disappear into it.

Finally, I reached across and squeezed Keyanna's hand. "One day...when the time's right...you'll get the truth. I promise you that. But tonight, just eat your food. You need strength. 'Cause life gon' ask a lot more questions than this."

Her jaw tightened, but she nodded, stabbing her fork into her pasta. "Fine."

Dinner went back to noise after that — but it wasn't normal anymore. The weight sat between us like a fourth plate nobody touched.

And I knew, deep down, the day I promised her would come. And when it did, it might burn us all.

CHAPTER

24

Last Chapter

The last door clanged open like a bell for the dead. CJ stepped through with a state duffel and twenty years of weight stitched into his shoulders. He stood there a moment, eyes shut, chin lifted into the sun like he had to relearn it. Air hit different out here—dirt and hot tar and cut grass and somebody's cologne blowing off a passing car. He swallowed hard. The world was loud. Alive. Disrespectfully bright.

"Clark!" a CO barked from behind the fence, like the concrete still owned his name.

CJ didn't turn. He rolled his neck until it popped and kept breathing. Two decades of concrete mornings, metal nights, countless nights of knives sharpening against the concrete, the thud of boots, the hush of men pretending not to cry—he felt all of it slipping off his skin like an old coat.

Then the phantom showed up.

She came in low and silent, big as a whale and just as smooth—the Rolls-Royce Wraith, midnight paint swallowing the sun, chrome Spirit of Ecstasy glinting like a private joke. Driver's door lifted. There she was, one leg out, heel striking pavement: Jasmine, red silk dress hugging wicked curves, a diamond cross catching fire at her throat. Shades down. Mouth a soft weapon with soft pink lips.

"Took you long enough," she said, voice like velvet with a razor stitched in.

CJ dropped the bag. For a half second he forgot he was supposed to be tough and just grabbed her, picked her clean off the ground. She laughed into his neck, surprised and soft, hands at his jaw like she was making sure the bones were real.

"You real," he breathed. "You still real."

"Always," she said. "Get in the car, king. The world's waitin'."

The Wraith door closed with that Rolls hush, like money telling secrets. He ran his finger across the wood veneer, the starlight headliner winking above like a private sky. He looked at Jas and smiled like a man tasting water for the first time.

"Damn," he said. "You really did it."

"I told you," she said, shifting in one smooth motion. "I don't do halfway."

The V-12 sighed. The prison shrank in the mirror like a bad rumor.

They cut onto the freeway and Atlanta spilled everywhere—cranes like iron trees, fresh glass towers, murals loud as sermons. CJ sat quiet, soaking, pupils huge like a kid in a planetarium.

"You hungry?" she asked.

"For everything," he said. Then, softer: "But yeah. Food first. Real food."

"I cooked," Jas said.

He looked at her sideways. "Since when you in the kitchen?"

"Since you got free," she said, smirking.

They rode in a pocket of silence that wasn't empty. CJ studied her stealthy—the clean lines of her cheekbones, the new steel in her eyes. She always had fire; now she had temperature control. A storm with a thermostat.

"You look...expensive," he said. "But it ain't just the clothes."

"It's peace," she said. "Costs more than Dior."

"You happy?" he asked.

She tapped the wheel twice, thought about lying, decided not to. "I'm efficient."

"Mm." He knew that answer from the old days. It meant not yet.

They rolled past a city bus stop and a boy stared at the Wraith like the car might blink. CJ remembered being that boy. He remembered being the man the boy stared at. He touched the window with two fingers. Cool glass, warm palm. "Everything changed," he muttered.

"Not everything," Jas said, and laid her hand over his.

He didn't pull away.

No valet. No doorman show. She took him to a building you wouldn't notice unless you knew exactly where to look—Buckhead-adjacent, trees guarding the entrance, cameras pointed outward, not inward. Private elevator. Key fob. The kind of quiet that had a backbone.

Inside, the place breathed clean: linen, leather, a faint ribbon of vanilla. CJ set the duffel down like it might break the floor, then stood still as the room gave itself to him. Neutral stone. Wide couch. A wall of glass pouring Atlanta into the living room. On a console table, a box with A MA MANIÉRE embossed in silver.

"Go ahead," Jas said.

He lifted the lid. Inside: triple-white Forces, crisp as new snow. Size 11½.

"How you remember my—"

"I don't forget," she said, already in the kitchen, wrist turning a gold faucet on, water hitting a crystal glass like rain. "Bathroom's down the hall. Bedroom's at the end. Closet's empty 'cept what's yours. We'll fill it. Slowly."

He opened a second box: a navy suit, soft as a secret. On the dresser: a leather wallet, a key with a satin ribbon, and a phone, already set up. Wallpaper: a photo of the Atlanta skyline at dusk.

He swallowed around something heavy. "You did all this?"

"Some of it," she said, plating steak and lobster like a quiet flex. "Rest can wait."

CJ drifted down the hall. In the bathroom, he flicked the light and stared at himself like a stranger he almost liked. Jaw thicker. Eyes older, but not dull. A faint scar he didn't used to have, but prison fights would leave its mark. He turned the water on full hot and watched steam climb.

When he came out, she was waiting at the table, red silk crossed at the thighs, wine breathing in big-bellied glasses. The plates looked like indulgence carved into shapes.

He sat. Didn't touch a bite for five seconds. Then gave up pretending and ate like gratitude had hands.

"Slow down," she laughed. "It ain't your last meal."

"Feels like my first," he said, not looking up.

They talked around full mouths and twenty years. What prison did to time. What money did to noise. Who fell off. Who glowed up. Who you could still trust. The conversation moved like two people carrying a couch—awkward, then in rhythm, then easy.

By the time he chased the last macaroni curl with his fork, his shoulders had dropped an inch. The city in the glass had gone purple.

"Come here," Jas said.

He did.

They didn't go straight to the bedroom. Not yet. She led him to the window first, pressed his palm to the cool glass.

"Look," she said, mouth near his ear. "No fences."

He didn't realize he'd been holding his breath until he heard it leave him. He closed his hand into a fist and left a fog print on the glass like a ghost trying to get back in.

She turned him around with two fingers under his chin. No rush. No apology. Just that soft authority she wore like a fragrance. "You good?"

"Better than good," he said. Then, because he couldn't help himself: "You ain't ask me nothing."

"Should I?"

"Like...what I did. What I didn't."

She studied him, a long, even look. "I know enough. The rest isn't urgent."

Something unknotted behind his ribs. The coil that prison ties around a man's spine loosened a click.

"You still mine?" he asked, a little drunk off freedom.

Her smile was wicked and careful at once. "Try me."

She took his hand and walked him down the hall, lights dimming on a sensor like the house itself knew how to behave. In the bedroom, the bed waited wide, sheets turned back in a hotel fold. Her perfume lived in the air like a promise.

He reached to touch her and she stepped away—not no, just not yet—and lifted her dress zipper with two slow fingers. Red silk whispered to the floor. He stared. Not like a boy seeing skin for the first time. Like a man remembering where he left his vow.

"Jas," he said, voice low.

"CJ," she answered, stepping into him, one hand at his chest, the other sliding his shirt off his shoulders like regret.

"What's the rules?" he asked, because prison had taught him to ask before he took.

"Only one," she said, mouth brushing his. "Remember me."

"Easy," he said, and kissed her like a man who'd been living on rationed air.

They hit the mattress in pieces—his laugh, her breath, a scatter of buttons and a soft curse when a cufflink refused to play along. He rolled, she rolled back, that tug-of-war they'd always loved coming back like muscle memory. The city hummed on the other side of the glass, a long electric chord under everything.

She straddled him slow, palms on his chest, weight settling like she was claiming territory. His hands traced the map of her—shoulders to waist to the notch of her hip—memorizing, not taking. She shivered and leaned down, kissing him quiet, deepening until the kiss turned into language.

"Still feels like home?" she whispered against his mouth.

"Feels like I never left," he said, voice wrecked.

She moved with a rhythm that was more than lust—patient, exact, tuned to the sound of his breath changing. He answered with his hands and his mouth, that husky laugh cutting loose when she surprised him, that old growl in his throat when she didn't. She opened her legs with ease to give him the go ahead for him to enter. His wood hard like his first erection in years. Her breath broke a silence, he would enter her walls soft and gentle like it was precious. Her lips met his lips, both tongues meeting each other like a dance on the ballroom floor.

Their rhythm met each other with passion and grace. Her titties bounced back and forth with every stroke. His cheeks clinched tight with every thrust of motion inside her.

She dug her nails inside his skin letting him know, that was his pussy and nobody else.

He answered, "Shit, Shit, Damn this pussy good".

Her eyes closed while her head leaned back. "Fuck me CJ. This your pussy."

His hands grabbed her throat hard but gentle just like she liked it. "Ahhh, Ahhh" her legs began to shake with the motion of a level 9 earthquake. "I'm cummin, I'm cummin" she said soft but loud enough to bounce off the walls. Her release was pure, seconds later he released into her 2 decades of pleasure he missed out on.

"God, I missed you," he said, and there was nothing hard about it.

"I know," she said, and there was nothing soft about it.

Heat stacked, breath stacked, the room braided itself around them. When it crested, it did it honest—no performance, no mask—just two bodies remembering how to be one thing for a minute. She clutched at his shoulders and broke like a wave; he held her steady and went right after, a rough exhale, eyes squeezed shut like prayer.

Silence landed heavy and sweet. Her cheek on his chest. His heartbeat slowing under her ear. The city washed the windows with moving light.

He threaded his fingers through her hair and kissed the top of her head. "Say it," he murmured.

She smiled into his skin. "You're home."

"And you're mine," he said, more habit than threat.

She didn't answer. She lifted her head, studied his face in the dark, then slipped off the bed and padded to the window, bare feet whispering on wood. The skyline put diamonds in her eyes. She stood there, silhouette and storm, then turned and crawled back under the sheets like nothing had changed.

"Sleep," she said, settling into the hollow of his shoulder. "Tomorrow's big."

"For what?" he yawned, already losing the fight.

"New clothes," she said. "New cut. New keys."

He sighed, satisfied, and slid under.

Jas stayed awake, eyes open, counting breaths until his turned regular. She reached for the nightstand, picked up the leather wallet she'd bought him, and ran her thumb down the edge like she was filing something invisible. In the glass, the city kept blinking. Behind her, CJ slept with a smile that looked like a truce.

She kissed two fingers and touched them to his temple. "Rest up, king," she whispered. "The show starts soon."

The Wraith slept in the garage like a black animal. The warehouse keys sat in her bag. Somewhere across town, a space was being dressed for joy that wasn't really joy. The clock on the stove slid from 2:12 to 2:13.

Jas finally closed her eyes.
The storm didn't.

CJ leaned back in the passenger seat of the
Wraith, fresh haircut still smelling like talc,
chain heavy against his chest. His laugh rattled
the car. "Damn, baby. You really rollin' me out
red carpet style, huh? You think a nigga forgot
how to party?"

Jas gripped the wheel tighter than she
needed to. "Ain't no red carpet. This Memphis
shit, remember? We don't roll, we stomp."

He chuckled, glancing at her. "Still talkin'
slick. I like that. Where we goin', though? You
all dressed like it's prom night."

She smirked. "Surprise."

He leaned back, spreading his arms wide.
"Shit, I love surprises. As long as they come
with liquor, weed, and some pussy on the side."

"Close your eyes," she said, smooth as
syrup.

"What?"

"I said close 'em. Better yet..." She pulled
the blindfold from the console, black silk,
folded neat. She dangled it like bait. "You trust
me?"

CJ stared, grin wide. "Hell yeah. Who else I got?" He let her tie it, laughing. "You try somethin', Jas, I swear—"

"Shut up," she cut him off, tight. "Enjoy the ride."

He sat back, blindfold snug, smile plastered across his face. "Yeah, I feel it. Nigga back. Streets gon' love me."

The warehouse swallowed them whole, bass from hidden speakers making the walls hum. Jas led him in slow, heels cracking against the concrete. He laughed, blindfolded, sniffing the air.

"Smell like loud and Henny already. You ain't slick, baby. Who here? Slim? Rico? Shit, tell me my old heads still—"

"Sit down," Jas said, pushing him into the heavy chair staged dead center.

He chuckled. "Oh, we kinky now? I ain't mad at it." He tugged at the straps, grinning. "Nigga fresh out and already gettin' tied up. Y'all bitches wild."

Leather bit his wrists as she cinched them tight. Ankles too. He shifted. "Damn, you strong as hell. You been hittin' the gym or some shit?"

"Be quiet," Jas said.

But he kept running his mouth. "Bet. Y'all gon' put some stripper on me, huh? Let her grind me to death. I can live with that."

Music swelled — not the party anthem he expected but something darker. Bass low, humming like a storm underfoot. His smile faltered a notch.

Jas stood in front of him, pulling the blindfold slow. Light hit his eyes. He blinked, squinted...and froze.

No crowd. No homies. No bottles. Just shadows. Just silence.

And her.

Phantum mask glinting under a single overhead light, the white half-face gleaming sharp against her skin. He sucked air through his teeth.

"What the fuck is this?" His voice cracked, a nervous laugh following. "You playin', right? Jas? Baby girl?"

She tilted her head, mask catching the light.

He tugged at the straps. "Yo, stop fuckin' around. Where everybody at?"

Her answer was low, cold, steel in Memphis drawl. "Right where they s'posed to be. Gone."

His grin dropped. "Jas..."

"Don't call me that," she snapped. The mask tilted closer. "You lookin' at Phantum now."

From the shadows, small footsteps. A figure stepped into the light.

Keyanna.

Barely twenty. Fierce eyes, curls wild, body stiff with fear but fists balled anyway. She looked like Jas's mirror, just younger, unburned.

CJ's face broke. "What the—who the fuck is this?"

Jas's voice didn't waver. "Your blood. KeeKee's baby. The one you left in this world after beatin' her mama to death."

CJ blinked hard, shook his head, spat, "Nah. You lyin'. You lyin' like fuck."

Keyanna's voice cracked, sharp and trembling. "You my daddy? You the nigga that left my mama in the dirt?"

CJ's chest rose fast. "No, no, baby girl, listen—"

"Shut up!" Jas barked, slapping him across the face with the pistol so hard his head snapped sideways.

Blood sprayed, spit trailing from his mouth. He coughed, eyes watering. "Goddamn! Jas—Phantum—whatever the fuck—you gon' hit me like that?"

"SHUT THE FUCK UP," she repeated, mask inches from his face.

Keyanna's lips trembled, tears cutting down her cheeks. "You... you really did that?"

CJ sagged against the straps, blood dripping from his lip. He spit, red hitting the floor. His chest heaved, breath rough.

"I fucked up," he croaked, voice breaking. "I was young, wild, high as hell... I ain't mean for KeeKee to go out like that. I ain't mean it, Keyanna."

Jas's eyes narrowed behind the mask. "Mean it or not, you did it. You made her a ghost. You made this girl grow up with nothin' but questions. You don't get to rewrite shit now."

CJ's tears came fast, ugly, his shoulders jerking. "Please. Please, Jas. Don't do this. Don't let her—don't make her see me like this. I'm beggin' you."

Keyanna's whole body shook. She raised the gun Jas had laid in her hands earlier, arms trembling, finger flirting with the trigger.

"Daddy..." she whispered, word tasting like poison.

CJ sobbed. Loud. No pride left. "Baby girl, I swear, I'm sorry. I'm so sorry. If I could trade places with your mama, I would. Just...please don't...don't pull that on me. Not you."

The warehouse air felt thick, stale with dust and bass humming under the floor. CJ's chest rose and fell fast, wrists yanking at the straps like he could break free by will alone.

Jas circled him slow, Phantum mask gleaming, pistol swinging loose in her hand. Her voice came sharp, steady, Memphis dripping off every word.

"You don't even fuckin' know, do you?"

CJ blinked, blood trailing down his chin. "Know what? Jas, baby, please—"

"Stop callin' me that," she snapped. "KeeKee. My sister. My blood. You ain't even know we was family, did you?"

His whole body jerked like he'd been slapped harder than the pistol already gave him. "What?!"

"Yeah, nigga," Jas spat. "Sisters. Same mama. Same house. While you was out here beatin' her and leavin' her for dead, I was the one buryin' her spirit every damn day. You ain't kill just some girl. You killed my fuckin' sister."

CJ's face cracked wide open, terror and disbelief mixing. "No...nah, you lyin'. You playin' wit' me. KeeKee? Y'all was—" He shook his head violently. "Fuck, I ain't know! Jas, on my mama, I ain't know she was your kin!"

"You ain't care either," Jas cut in, voice like glass breaking. "All you saw was a mouth ready

297

to talk. She told me before she died—you put hands on her, got her pregnant, then she said she was gon' take it to the cops, blow the whole block open. You couldn't let that happen, could you?"

CJ shook his head, veins bulging in his neck, spit flying. "I ain't—I ain't mean for her to die! I just wanted her quiet, that's it! I was young, high, mad—"

"Shut the fuck up," Jas hissed, slamming the pistol into his jaw so hard blood spit from his mouth. He coughed, gagging, tears streaming now.

Keyanna's voice cut in, sharp and raw. "So it's true. All them nights I heard whispers, all them stories—the boyfriend did it. It was you."

CJ's head snapped toward her, eyes wild, red leaking from his mouth. "Baby girl, please—listen to me—"

"Don't fuckin' call me that!" Keyanna screamed, tears streaking down her cheeks. "You killed my mama. You let me grow up hearin' my whole life she died 'cause of some nigga she trusted—and it was you! You!"

She stepped forward, hand shaking, then swung the gun across his face. The crack echoed. CJ's head snapped sideways, teeth clattering against concrete as blood sprayed.

"You ain't shit!" she sobbed, spitting straight in his face.

CJ gagged, coughing, spitting red. The chair creaked under him. "I didn't know, Keyanna, I swear to God, I didn't know she was my—my blood, I didn't know you was mine! If I had—fuck—if I had known—"

"You would've still killed her," Jas cut in, voice cold, mask glowing under the single bulb. "Don't lie now. She was a threat. And you always killed threats."

He broke then. Ugly crying. Shoulders jerking, chest heaving, snot and blood mixing on his face. "I'm sorry! I'm fuckin' sorry, alright? KeeKee, you, Jas—all of y'all—I fucked up, I fucked everything up! Please, Jas! Don't let her shoot me! Don't let my daughter—"

"She your daughter now?" Jas hissed. "After eighteen years of silence? After she had to raise herself off scraps of rumors?"

CJ sobbed harder. "Give me one chance! Just one! Please!"

Keyanna's hands shook around the pistol, but her eyes burned hot. "You had your chance, nigga. My mama begged for her life. You ain't listen. Why the fuck should I?"

CJ whimpered, voice high, broken. "Please, baby... I ain't never begged no one in my life, but I'm beggin' you now. Forgive me. Don't pull that trigger."

Jas stepped behind her niece, steadying her shoulders, whispering low but sharp enough to slice. "Ghosts cry good when hell's waitin'. Don't let his tears fool you."

Keyanna's breath came fast, ragged. She pressed the barrel harder into CJ's forehead, tears dripping onto his bloody face.

"I should kill you right now," she spat. "For every fuckin' night I wondered why I ain't have a mama. For every whisper that broke me. For every lie."

Her finger trembled on the trigger. The warehouse buzzed with nothing but fear, rage, and ghosts finally named.

The warehouse got quiet like even the walls stopped breathing. The bass that had been humming low cut off, leaving nothing but the sound of blood dripping from CJ's busted lip onto the concrete. Plink... plink... plink.

Jas stood masked, still as a shadow, pistol in hand. Keyanna stood trembling, but her arms were locked straight, barrel pressed against CJ's forehead.

CJ's chest rose fast, ragged, like a man drowning on dry land. His eyes darted between the mask and the girl. His girl.

"Please," he croaked, voice shredded. "Keyanna... baby girl... I didn't mean it. I was young, I was high, I was stupid. KeeKee—she said she was gonna run to the cops, shut the whole operation down. I snapped. I didn't mean to kill her. I swear on my soul."

Keyanna's teeth clenched so hard her jaw shook. Tears streaked her face, but her grip didn't falter. "You swear on your soul? Nigga, you ain't even got one. You left my mama in the dirt like she wasn't shit. You left me with nothin'. And now you wanna beg?"

CJ sobbed, shoulders jerking, spit and blood mixing as he coughed. "Please, don't do this! Jas—Phantum—don't let her do this! Don't let my daughter kill me!"

Jas' voice sliced through the silence, cold and final. "Don't look at me, ghost. This her decision. You took her mama. Tonight she decides if you still get to breathe."

The room seemed to stretch. Time slowed. Keyanna's breath came in sharp bursts, the pistol steady against his skull. Her finger trembled on the trigger.

CJ whispered, broken, "Baby, please..."

Keyanna blinked through tears, the world blurring around her until all she saw was him — this man who gave her life and ripped it away in the same motion.

The air got heavy. Silence pressed on them all. Even the shadows seemed to lean in.

Then —
BOOM.

The shot cracked like thunder. CJ's head snapped back, blood and bone spraying against the warehouse wall. His body slumped, lifeless, still strapped to the chair.

Keyanna's chest heaved, "FUCKK YOOOOUUU!," gun slipping from her hand, clattering on the floor. Her scream ripped out, half pain, half release, echoing in the hollow space.

Jas caught her before she fell, pulling her close, whispering through the mask, "It's over, baby. Ghosts don't get to haunt us no more."

The room went dead quiet again, except for the ringing in their ears and the drip of blood sliding down concrete.

CJ was gone. For good.

The gun smoke still hung in the warehouse, sharp in the air, mixing with blood and burnt powder. Keyanna shook in Jas's arms, her face buried in Phantum's chest. Jas rocked her slow, whispering, "You strong, baby. You did what had to be done."

CJ's body sagged in the chair, blood dripping in steady lines, pooling at his feet. The ghost was gone.

The steel door creaked open, and Diego stepped in, his brother right behind him. No shock on their faces. Just calm. Just business.

Diego's eyes found Jas. "It's done?"

Jas gave a single nod. "It's done."

He crossed to the chair, pulling gloves tight, and leaned over CJ's lifeless form. "We'll make it look like he ran. Parolee back to his old shit, couldn't take the leash, dipped out. Streets'll eat that story alive."

His brother dragged a heavy tarp across the floor, unrolling it with a smack. Together, they moved quick, practiced. Blood wiped. Shell casing pocketed. CJ's body wrapped and zipped like he was never even there.

Keyanna turned her face away, gagging. Jas held her tighter, whispering, "Don't look, baby. We movin' forward now."

Two nights later, I sat across from Tika in the condo. My mask was gone, face tired but steady. Tika's eyes were wide, searching.

"So where he at? I thought CJ was gon' be home for good. You said the lawyer—"

I cut her off with a shake of the head, voice low, cracking just enough to sound like hurt. "He ran, Tika. Couldn't handle the streets watchin' him. Couldn't handle me. He just... left."

Tika's hand flew to her mouth. "What? He left you? After all them years? After you held him down?"

I let the tears slide slow down my cheeks, real and fake all at once. "Yeah. Left me hurt all over again. Nigga was never who I thought he was."

Tika shook her head, anger sparking. "Fuck him then. Fuck him."

"Yeah," I whispered. "Fuck him."

Later that night, on the balcony with Tika, Miami lights were on my mind.

"I'm done wit' this shit," voice firm. "CJ's gone. Ghosts buried. I'm movin' to Miami wit' Diego. New life, new money, no more lookin' over my shoulder."

Tika blinked, shocked. "Miami? Just like that?"

"Yeah...Just like that. And you can come too. Condo, clothes, sun, no more drama. Just us livin' the life we used to dream about."

Tika stared at her, tears brimming, then let out a shaky laugh. "Bitch...you for real?"

"For real," I said, pulling her close. "You my sister, blood or not. I ain't leavin' you behind."

Tika nodded slow, looking out at the night sky. "Alright then. Miami it is."

By dawn, Diego had ourr bags packed and cars waiting. The Rolls sat curbside, trunk heavy with designer luggage and crypto wallets hidden deeper than TSA would ever check.

Keyanna sat in the backseat, face pale but eyes sharp now, like she'd aged ten years overnight. I climbed in beside her, squeezing her hand. "We the ghosts now, baby. But we ghosts with power."

Diego slid behind the wheel, engine purring. "Miami, here we come."

The city lights blurred in the rearview as they pulled away. Behind them, Atlanta slept — and CJ's ghost slept with it.

Phantum wasn't just a name. It was survival. And in Miami, ghosts didn't hide — they ruled.

Epilogue

The night Jasmine left Atlanta, the city went quiet. Even the traffic seemed to move softer, like it knew something powerful had slipped away. She didn't leave a note, didn't look back, didn't owe anyone her explanation. Atlanta had seen enough of her — the love, the blood, the headlines. All it needed now was her silence.

Her name was still on everyone's lips though, whispered in barbershops, clubs, and late-night phone calls. Some said she ran to Miami. Others said she vanished for good. But those who knew her best understood — Jasmine didn't run. She transformed.

While their flight disappeared into the clouds, another story was beginning to rise. Keyanna stood on the balcony of the new condo where the skyline was orange from the bright sun hitting the water. The memory of the night before fresh on her mind. The cracked mask sat on the glass table, the same one that hid Jasmine's sins and crowned her power.

Keyanna stared at it for a long time, her reflection split down the middle by the fracture that ran through it. The mask looked fragile, but it felt alive — humming with the echoes of everything Jasmine had been. With a slow breath, she reached out and lifted it.

"You ran your course, Jas," she whispered, voice low but certain. "But me? I'm just getting started, Miami about to be my city."

The city lights flickered across her face as she slid the mask over her skin. It didn't feel stolen. It felt right. Like the mask had been waiting for her all along. Down below, the streets of Miami heartbeat roared — engines, sirens, laughter, sin. The same chaos that once crowned Jasmine now called to Keyanna. And she was ready to answer.

While Jasmine was relocating looking for redemption, a new Phantum was being born in the same mask she just tried to leave behind. The legend hadn't died — it had just changed faces.

Acknowledgments

C Clark: I'd like to thank God, and my supporters who follow me through thick and thin. My mother (Marilyn) who is always in my corner. My sister for praying over me and having my back. Thank you to the entire team CCLARKMEDIA who made this book possible.

Jasmine: I'd like to thank God and all of my family friends and supporters. The Phantasizers who have been rocking with on all of my platforms. I want to thank you from the bottom of my heart, and tell you I love you all.

REBORN IN
THE CITY

chapter

9

A Celebrity in the Making

By the time my name started ringing bells, I was still technically grounded—on house arrest. No trips, no out-of-state bookings, no fancy location shoots. But one loophole in the system kept me breathing: I had no curfew. That meant I could move around the city all day and all night, as long as I stayed within Atlanta. And I made every second of that freedom count. Every moment was just that more important.

I treated the city like a networking playground. If there was a party, I was at the door.

If there was a model meetup, I found a way in. I wasn't just out here to stunt—I was studying. Watching how people moved. Learning who had influence and who was all cap. I was building something, and I needed to understand the game from every angle.

Back then, Instagram wasn't what it is now. Facebook was cool, but the real networking happened face-to-face. So I printed flyers. I made business cards. I asked clients to tag me on Myspace, on blogs, in Yahoo groups—wherever they had reach. Every photo I took was more than just a snapshot. It was marketing. I watermarked my images with my logo. If your favorite model posted a picture, chances are it had "C CLARK PHOTOGRAPHY" stamped right on it. I had to show them who I was and what I was presenting.

My work started traveling faster than I could. People who'd never met me knew my name. I'd walk into clubs and hear, "Yo, you that camera dude, right?" Bartenders, promoters, DJs—they all wanted to work with me. And I never said no. I shot for free sometimes just to get my foot in the room, just to show I was serious. I'd shoot behind-the-scenes at music videos, album release parties, stripper battles—anything that had lights and energy, I was there.

At one point, I was shooting four to five models a day and, sometimes out of my home it would be 10. Even in rented spaces sometimes trying to upgrade my look. I created mini sets with furniture, props, painted walls. I learned to make a scene look rich, even if the space was broke. That was my superpower. Making people look like stars. That was my specialty over most other photographers.

Models started hitting me up from across the city. Not just for pretty pictures—but for direction. They saw how my images got more attention, how they helped other women grow their pages, get bookings, get paid. I was giving them sauce and didn't even realize it yet. I was teaching branding before I had the language for it.

And let's not lie—the lifestyle was intoxicating. I was surrounded by beauty, by ambition, by women who were bold and unapologetic about their image. I kept it professional, always. But being in that environment? It pushed me. It made me want to sharpen my eye, improve my skill, stay ahead of the competition. Because if I didn't, somebody else would.

One of my biggest moves during this time was organizing themed photoshoot days. I'd rent a luxury apartment or event space, schedule 10–15 models back-to-back, offer hair and makeup, and run the whole thing like a production studio. I called them "Power Shoots." They'd sell out in hours. And I wasn't just shooting—I was coaching, curating outfits, directing poses, creating content packages.

Eventually, club promoters started calling me. They wanted me to shoot their flyers, their bottle girls, their events. I was becoming the go-to guy for visual storytelling in the urban scene. I started wearing branded T-shirts that said "BOOK ME NOW" with my IG and number printed in bold. Wherever I went, I was marketing.

But behind all that motion, I was still on edge. That court case was still hanging over my head like a cloud. Any day could be the day I got that call. That fear pushed me even harder. I wanted to make as much noise as possible before the system tried to silence me again. I was building a legacy in real-time, and every client, every shoot, every edited file was a brick in the foundation.

Looking back, I realize that phase of my life wasn't just about photography—it was about resilience. I was learning how to turn limitations into leverage. How to outwork doubt. How to take every little win and multiply it.

That's when I knew—I wasn't just taking pictures anymore. I was making my name mean something. Something bigger than what the eyes could see.

People started saying my name in rooms I hadn't even walked in yet. I'd see my work reposted on modeling forums, nightlife blogs, even in barbershops where dudes were debating who had the baddest shoot. That's when it hit me—I wasn't just local anymore. I was becoming a brand. A brand with a good sounding name and no games being played behind it.

But it wasn't all smooth. With popularity comes pressure. Models expected me to deliver magic every time. There were times I doubted myself—when the lighting wasn't right, when I was editing until 4 a.m., when I second-guessed the angles I chose. I didn't have a team yet. I was the shooter, editor, customer service, promoter, and accountant. If a client was late, I had to reschedule ten others. If something went wrong, it all came back to me.

I was building in real time with no playbook. But that taught me grit. Taught me accountability. Taught me how to move like a boss even when I didn't feel like one yet.

I also started paying attention to how models presented themselves online. Some had amazing looks but poor captions. Some had great presence but didn't post enough. I started giving advice after every shoot: "Here's how you should drop this pic." "Post this at 8 p.m., your followers are most active then." "Pair this photo with a quote that makes people stop scrolling."

Before I even realized it, I was consulting. Brand coaching. Creating strategy. These women started trusting me not just with their image—but with their whole business. And I didn't take that lightly.

The more I helped others, the more I grew. I started offering packages that included marketing tips, editing breakdowns, reposting schedules. I told them: "You're not just a model, you're a brand. You need consistency, narrative, identity." I helped them pick names, colors, taglines. I helped them dream bigger.

And slowly, my business stopped being about just photography. It became a machine. A content studio. A launchpad for people trying to rebrand themselves.

But the grind took a toll too. I missed time with my daughter, Niya. I missed birthdays. I was so locked into building, I sometimes forgot to live. That's the part they don't show on social media— the fatigue, the loneliness, the constant pressure to be on.

Still, I knew I was doing something right when people started calling me the "go-to" in Atlanta. When folks would say, "If you ain't shot with C Clark, are you even serious?" That meant something.

And through it all, Ms. R stayed in my corner. She held me down through the long nights, the canceled dates, the stress. She watched me transform from a street kid with a camera into a man with purpose. She saw the ups and downs, and she never waivered. She reminded me why I started and why I couldn't stop.

When I look back on those days now, I don't just see photos—I see proof. Proof that even with limitations, you can build a name that rings. That even with a record, you can craft a reputation. That even while fighting a case, you can fight for your dream at the same time.

I became a celebrity in my own right—not for being flashy, but for being consistent. For showing up, over and over, when most would've folded. That's the real flex.

One thing I learned through that climb was this: fame without foundation is fragile. I didn't want to just be known—I wanted to be remembered. I wanted my name to carry weight long after the flash faded.

I started planting seeds for the future. Mapping out ideas for a digital platform, studying brand licensing, planning courses for creators who wanted to learn what I had taught myself. My mind was expanding past the lens. I saw that content was currency—and I had a vault full of it.

Every shoot became a case study. Every edit, a resume line. Every satisfied client, a brand ambassador. I wasn't just building a business—I was shaping a movement.

Being on house arrest forced me to build inward. To craft a world that didn't rely on access but on creativity. And that taught me a lesson I still carry today: you don't need a passport to make an impact—you just need purpose and precision.

The streets might've made me, but the camera refined me. And as the city kept whispering my name louder, I knew—C CLARK wasn't just a man with a camera anymore.

He was a brand. A boss. A blueprint.

And the hustle was just getting started.